Thanks For taking
care of my wife!

M. R.
AuthorMike

White Ash
A Collection of Fiction

By
Michael Aloisi

www.AuthorMikeInk.com

ISBN: 0-9845801-0-7
ISBN-13: 978-0-9845801-0-1
Library of Congress Control Number: 2010907966

This book is a work of fiction. People, places, events and situations are the product of the author's imagination. Any resemblance to actual persons, living or dead, or historical events is purely coincidental.

First Published by *AuthorMike Ink*, 6/8/2010

www.AuthorMikeInk.com

AuthorMike Ink and its logo are trademarked by *AuthorMike Ink Publishing*.

Printed in the United States of America

**Also By
Michael Aloisi**

*Fifty Handfuls
Mr. Bluestick*

For All My Students,
Past, Present and Future

Table of Contents

Indicates previously unreleased stories.

Table of Contents

Inspirations

INTRODUCTION

For over a year now, I have published one short story a month on my personal website, AuthorMike.com, to give my readers something new to read all year long. Knowing a lot of my readers do not like to read on a computer and that a lot of them like to collect books, I have decided to turn those stories into a collection. I have compiled sixteen months of shorts along with four original, never-before-published stories within these pages.

Being a consummate teacher, I have decided to do something unique with this book. In the *Inspiration* section, I have included short essays about the inspirations for each of the stories. I did this for two reasons. As a teacher of the craft of writing, I find it invaluable for students to see where a writer's ideas come from—how they take their everyday life along with their imagination and turn it into prose. Secondly, I constantly get bombarded with people asking, *where did you come up with that?* This section will answer the casual reader's question as well as give some insight into the writing process.

I sincerely hope you enjoy *White Ash*, and I invite you to stop by my website to drop me a line and let me knew what you thought of it. While there, you'll be able to read new short stories and learn about how you can invite me to your local book club or library.

Read and Write Often
AuthorMike

WHITE ASH

I was twenty-three when Janice and I planted the tree. We had just moved into the house, our first house, and we wanted something to make the yard *ours*. We went to a nursery and touched, smelled, and examined dozens of trees. When Janice saw the small White Ash, she knew it was the one for our tree belt. The store manager tried to talk us out of it, saying it wasn't mature enough to plant and probably wouldn't survive. Janice loved a challenge and wanted to prove the man wrong, and she did. Every day she took care of that tree like it was her child. After that first year, it had rooted and Janice didn't need to give it attention any more. Just as with a child, Janice let it go, to grow and live on its own. Every now and then when she was out gardening, I would see her staring at it and smiling. She was proud of the tree and loved it dearly.

Forty-one years later the tree is massive. It sits, stoic, as if it had been there for centuries. It's so big and beautiful that when guests come to our house for the first time, we tell them, *Just look for the house with the great white ash on the tree belt.* No one misses our house. Besides being a directional landmark and having to rake up its leaves every year, I never thought of the tree. Until now. Now it is all I can think of. I keep thinking of the day we picked it. If we had picked a different tree forty years ago, would all of this still have happened? I keep thinking of the spot on the tree belt where we dug the earth to bury its roots. I wanted it three feet over, but Janice was stubborn. I gave in when she kissed me and let her plant it where she wanted. If I had put my foot down and planted it where I wanted, or even if we compromised and planted it between the two spots, would Janice be dead today?

It was one-thirty-nine in the morning exactly when I jumped out of bed, thinking the world was ending. The noise was sudden and deafening. With sleep still dancing at the edges of my consciousness I looked around the bedroom and saw nothing was disturbed. The only thing moving was the decorative glass ball that held a delicate glass tree inside. Janice loved it; it reminded her of the White Ash, so she hung it in our window. It swayed ever so gently. Staring at it, I feared we were having an earthquake. My heart started to thump as I wondered how I would get Janice to a safe place in case there were aftershocks. The doorway was only ten feet away, but getting her out of bed was a production. In the morning, it took me fifteen minutes using a hospital lift to get her into her wheelchair; how was I supposed to do it in a matter of seconds? As I was about to race to Janice and drag her out by all means necessary, I heard a scream outside.

Janice's finger pointed to the window without her hand lifting off the bed. My gut tightened as I heard another cry. Peeking through the blinds, the glass ball touched my temple. It was cool and soothing, I almost wanted to close my eyes and let it roll over my forehead, as if I knew what I was about to see would scar my mind forever. The front yard is usually dark; the White Ash blocks the solo streetlight, casting a massive shadow on our house. Tonight, though, the yard was lit up with flickering orange light. It took my eyes a few seconds to focus. When they did, I saw a car wrapped around the forty-year-old tree. I let go of the slats in the curtain, as if it wouldn't exist if I couldn't see it.

"*Go*," Janice whispered. She hardly talked anymore; it pained her too much to do so. I wanted nothing more than to call the police and stay in the house, but Janice's voice ignited me. Before I knew it, I was sloppily dressed with a fire extinguisher in one hand and my cell in the other. I had an operator on the phone by the time I got to my front lawn. She had enough information, so I hung up, stuffed the cell in my pocket, and readied the extinguisher. Just as I was about to spray, the passenger side back door opened. A girl—a baby to me, really, just nineteen or so—fell to the grass, then jumped up screaming. Her arms stuck out in front of her like a zombie. One arm was normal with a white sleeve and pink manicured nails; the other arm was missing from the elbow down, a mere stump, dribbling blood between its powerful spurts. I looked from the fire to the girl, not knowing which one to attend to first. When I looked to her face, I thought of my own daughter—she was that age once, years ago. I had to help her.

Grabbing the stump of her arm I raised it up, pulled the belt off of my robe and wrapped the fuzzy blue cloth tightly as I could around the mangled limb. I knew nothing about first aid, but they did that in all the movies. I then helped her to my front steps and sat her down.

3

"How many are in the car?" I tried to ask several times, but she could do nothing but cry and mumble words that made no sense. As I ran back to the fire extinguisher, I saw other neighbors running out of their houses. Sadly, I did not hear sirens yet. With the nozzle in hand I sprayed the hood of the car, but the flames were too hot, probably burning off some combustible fluid. I threw the extinguisher aside and tried to get as close as I could to the car, to see inside, to see if I could help anyone else. To my horror, there were four more people inside. I knew instantly the two girls in the front were dead. The driver's head was…almost gone…and her hair…was on fire. The passenger was slumped forward, but I could tell by the bone protruding from the back of her neck that there was no way to save her. Swallowing hard, an image of my own two daughters posing for pictures in front of this tree flashed in my mind. I closed my eyes for a second, praying that when I looked in the back I would see movement, something to show me they were alive.

They were alive. They were stunned, but they looked fine. They had their seatbelts on. The one against the door was a young boy whose jean jacket was covered in blood, but not his; he stared down at it like it was going to attack him. The girl in the middle had her hands over her ears, her eyes shut while she hummed loudly. I reached in and grabbed her arm. I screamed that they had to get out, that the car was on fire, but they didn't hear me. I had to remove the seat belts from both of them. I pulled out the girl with relative ease. My neighbor, Chuck, who arrived wearing boxers and nothing else, helped me pull out the guy, who seemed to not want to leave.

With the three passengers sitting on the grass and neighbors starting to gather, I finally heard sirens in the background. I looked down at my white shirt and pajama pants. My robe had somehow come off during all of this and one of the girls had it over her shoulders. I was covered in shades of red and smears of black. Everyone that could be saved was out, yet I still had this overwhelming urge to keep helping. I spun around several times, seeing if I could help anywhere, but there was nothing more I could do. Turning back to the car, I watched the two bodies inside burn. Rubbing my eyes I focused my attention on my tree, our tree—Janice's tree. The fire was licking at it, the bark becoming singed. My breathing started to speed up. I wanted nothing more than to push the car away, put out the tree and save it—but I couldn't, just like I couldn't save Janice.

The first year that Janice took care of the White Ash, she had a fright. The leaves started to turn yellow and spotty in the middle of the summer. Janice did everything to try and save it. She went to the library and researched all the tree diseases she could find. She tried countless home remedies, but nothing seemed to work. I looked out the window one day to see her crying as she knelt by it. She didn't cover her face or wipe away her tears like she normally did. The tears merely ran off her cheek and fell into the freshly turned soil, to which she had just added her latest remedy. I let her cry that day. I don't know why, but I didn't go out and comfort her. When she came inside, I didn't mention it. I don't think she knew I had seen her cry. Two weeks later, the spots went away and the green came back. She attributed it to an eggshell and coffee ground cure she had whipped up. I liked to think it was because the tree felt the love she was giving it and willed itself to live.

With more and more rescue crews arriving, I slipped away from the crowd into my house. Inside the front door, I pulled the curtain down tight. Without even thinking, I stripped off all of my clothing right there at the door, scooped it up, tossed it in the kitchen trash, and headed down the hall. I wanted nothing more than to shower, to get the blood and ash off of me, but for some reason I walked right past the bathroom. Before I knew it, I was on my knees, my head buried in Janice's chest. I pulled her close, careful not to pull too much at the wires and tubes. I wanted her to pull me close, to wrap her body around me like she used to, but she couldn't do that. Her fingers were able to run through my hair, though. That simple gesture was enough for me to break down.

There were knocks on the door and the phone rang the rest of that night, but I ignored them. Every once in a while, I'd peek out the window to see the progress, hoping that everyone would be gone, that the tree would be fine and this would be just one big dream. Of course it wasn't. Each time I looked out, the crowd grew bigger and more vehicles arrived. Tow trucks, news crews, curious onlookers, and even a group of people praying. I wanted them all to go away. I wanted them to leave my yard and tree alone. I wanted the images of the poor girls out of my head.

At one point, when the sun was starting to rise, Janice wanted to see outside, to see what had happened. Since she could almost never get out of bed, I had devised a system of mirrors to let her see the front lawn whenever she wanted. I tried to talk her out of it, knowing if I opened the curtain, the reporters would flock to it like birds to feed, but I could never say no to Janice. Making sure the mirrors were set, I pulled up the blinds. The sky was a beautiful purple; I wanted to keep my eyes on that instead of looking down at the horror that was in my front yard. By this point, the bodies and the injured were gone, but the car was not. A tow truck was hooked to it and ready to start pulling it off the tree. The engine revved and the chains jangled as they pulled taut. I asked Janice if I could close the blinds. She shook her head no. So I stood there, with my hand wrapped around the string, eagerly waiting to let the slats fall.

The noise was horrible, even worse than the crash that woke us. The metal moaned and cried as it pulled from the tree. The truck screamed as it pulled harder and harder. And the worst... The worst was the sound of the wood tearing and pulling away from our beloved tree. For several minutes, these noises danced around our room, taunting us, until finally a loud slam announced the car was free. Reluctantly, I took my eyes off the sky—the calm, beautiful morning sky—and saw the White Ash. It looked like a drunken logger had gone at it with an axe. The bark was missing around the entire bottom quarter of the tree. Sporadic chunks were missing. The worst, though, was a three-foot gash where about a solid foot of wood was missing. Turning to Janice, I saw a tear roll down her cheek. I let the blinds slam shut.

I called out of work that morning. There were only a few months left until I retired, anyway, so I really didn't care. Besides, with Janice in her condition, they were used to me calling out. By nine, I had Janice cleaned and changed into her "day" clothing. I did my best to ignore what was going on outside. When I was ready, I took another peek—the car was gone and so were all the emergency crews, but there was still a small crowd of gawkers looking at the tree, touching, it. There was a baseball bat in the cellar; I thought about grabbing it and chasing the people off my lawn like they were vandals, but they weren't. They were merely concerned, curious citizens wanting a story to tell at work. Swallowing down my anger, I turned to Janice and forced a smile. She was having one of her bad days—I could always tell by her eyes.

It was one of those days when I didn't even need to ask her if she wanted to go into her chair or not. I could tell she was too weak. Watching her fall asleep, I felt exhaustion overtaking me. I wanted to get back into bed with her, to wrap my arm around her frail body and drift off to sleep, but for some reason I felt I had to stay up. In the kitchen, I sipped some cold coffee that the machine automatically spit out at seven. It was bitter and it stung my tongue, but I liked it. The pain in my mouth told me I was alive. The doorbell rang again; it was either a neighbor, reporter, or the cop back to get my statement. Without any thought, I pulled the chair to the hallway, climbed up on it, and tore the bell off the wall. The cost and pain of putting in a new one ran through my mind, but it didn't matter. I didn't want a bell disturbing Janice's sleep ever again.

Just before eleven, I finally felt it was safe to venture outside. As I put my hand on the door handle, the dead girl's smashed face flashed in my mind. I swallowed down the gore and opened the door. It was nice out. Warm, sunny. Not the way you would think a day that started off with tragedy would be like. The air felt good on my face; it always did when I left the stuffiness of Janice's room. I kept my eyes on the sky the first few steps. The world almost seemed normal. When I looked down, I saw that the lawn that Janice had taken so much pride in over the years, the greenest lawn on the street, was destroyed. The grass that had cost me thousands of dollars over the years to maintain was nothing but a mud bowl. The car, the emergency vehicles, and then the dozens of people tromping over it had destroyed our beautiful green blades. There were hardly any salvageable patches. The entire yard would have to be tilled and reseeded. This late in the season, it wouldn't grow until next spring. Janice would be devastated; she probably wouldn't even live long enough to see it grow back.

As I approached the tree, I noticed all the trash on my lawn. The gawkers had left breakfast sandwich wrappers and coffee cups strewn about. How could people be so careless about someone else's property? It wasn't only that. The emergency crews hadn't even bothered to clean up the glass; shards of metal and flecks of paint laid under the tree like some odd leftover confetti. I wanted to start cleaning it up, but I was so furious I didn't even know where to begin. How do you even clean glass out of dirt? I looked back at the house, wondering if I should check on Janice; she was never alone for long. Usually the day nurse would be by her side right now, phone in hand, waiting to call me when the "moment" came. If I lost her while cleaning up someone else's mess, I wouldn't be able to handle it. Trying to calm myself, I looked at the flowers at the base of the tree. There were three bouquets already and five candles. Two candles had crosses on them and another had Jesus with arms spread wide.

Jesus.

Religion used to be part of my life, mostly because Janice wanted it to be. I wasn't raised in a religious household, but she was and wanted our family to be that way. We took our kids to church every Sunday for eighteen years. When the kids moved out, we started to take off a Sunday here and there; we needed to rest our old bones on Sunday mornings rather than get up and get dressed. When Janice got sick, religion seemed to slip out the window unnoticed. I asked her a few times if she wanted to pray with me, but she shook her head no. Through it all, I still believed, even if I was angry—but now, now, I'm not sure. Why would God kill two young children and severe another's arm so brutally? Why would he put a tumor the size of a grapefruit next to the sweetest, kindest woman's heart? A kind God wouldn't put that tumor so close to the heart that it was inoperable. He wouldn't make it keep growing, restricting the heartbeats and putting pressure on her lungs. Religious people always say there is a reason for everything. Well, I'd like to hear the reason for today's accident and for my wife's having to suffer.

Leaning down, I blew out the three religious candles.

Our youngest daughter, Chloe, wanted a tree fort when she was nine. We had no suitable trees in the backyard—ours are mostly pine. The only tree that could possibly fit one was the White Ash in the front yard. I told her she couldn't have it there because, being right next to the street, it was too dangerous. She was so determined that she carried all my tools out of the garage one day and placed them by the tree. She didn't know what any of them did or how to use them, but she was going to try. Janice was the one who saw Chloe standing in the front yard, holding a level to the tree and nodding her head as if it were just right. Janice snapped three quick pictures before I went out and had to make my daughter cry. One of those pictures still hangs in the den.

The day was a waste. I didn't bother cleaning up much. I picked up the cups and paper, but the glass and metal shards I left for another day. At lunchtime, news crews showed up, set up across the street, and did their live reports. I put the television on for Janice to watch it. She bit her lower lip and watched the report in silence. When it was over, I shut it off and fluffed her pillow. When my head was above her face, she whispered to me, *I'd plant it again, even if I knew.* The comment took me by surprise. For one, she didn't talk much anymore—it hurt too much—and, for another, I couldn't believe she said it. Janice was someone who valued every life. Even bugs. She'd make me scoop up spiders and put them outside in the dead of winter because she couldn't stand the thought of them being killed. As I began to ask her why, her eyes fluttered asleep. I kissed her on the forehead and let her be.

11

In the late afternoon, she awoke with a loud scream. I was in the den trying to read, but really just staring at our family picture in front of the White Ash tree. Having never heard her make such a loud noise, I bolted to the room and fell to my knees by her side, wondering if this was the moment I was going to lose her. Before I could even assess what was wrong, I had tears in my eyes. Janice's mouth was wide open, her face was covered in sweat. It was going to happen. I wrapped my arms around her, pulled her to my chest, and told her with as much meaning as I could that I loved her.

Dream…bad, dream.

I let her go just enough to look at her face. A dream? Her breathing slowed down as I wiped the sweat off her brow. She seemed to be spooked, but all right. When I asked her what the dream was about, she licked her lips a few times and looked at the mirror. I hushed her and said everything was going to be alright. She didn't have to waste energy to tell me it was about the tree. As her eyes started to flutter again, I whispered to her that I would take care of the tree, that no matter what, I'd make sure it was fine.

On Janice's fiftieth birthday, I wrapped the White Ash's trunk entirely in gold and white crêpe paper. When the party ended, Janice was drunk. She snuck outside, barefoot, and stripped the tree of its unnatural casing. Circle by circle, she walked around the tree, taking off the crêpe paper, laughing and giggling the whole time. We made love on our deck that night, with strips of crêpe paper around our wrists.

Four camera crews showed up for the evening news. Our house was flooded with artificial light. The cameras zoomed in on our damaged tree and the shards of glass in the grass before interviewing the ever-growing crowd. Dozens of people showed up, all with candles in their hands and tears in their eyes. I wondered how many actually knew the girls and how many were just going along for the sympathy ride. I wanted nothing more than for these people to get off my lawn. The constant prayers and chatter were keeping Janice awake. She needed her sleep. I tried putting earplugs in her ears, but she kept shrugging me off. She asked several times for me to open the blinds so she could watch the vigil from the mirror, but I wouldn't do it. Ashamed, I even left the room so I wouldn't have to say no to her. In the den, I realized it was because *I* didn't want to see the vigil, not because I wanted to spare Janice the stress.

An hour later, I came back to apologize to Janice. Thankfully, she was asleep. I peeked out the window and saw that there were only what I assumed were family members left. A group of seven, four of whom were kneeling and sobbing. There was one man that stayed away from the group. He was on the opposite side of the tree, feeling the bark and crying silently. I knew from the look on his face that he was one of the fathers. Seeing his pain sent a quiver like I never felt before down my spine. I remember watching Chloe fall off her bike once. She was on the sidewalk and only fell onto the grass, but, to me, it seemed like she slipped off a cliff. It had taken my heart almost an hour to settle down. That feeling was not even a fraction of his suffering.

13

As the hours slipped by and I paced the house, I realized how exhausted I was. I needed sleep. Getting ready for bed, I took one last peek out the window only to find that everyone was gone. Only the mess, along with the memorial of flowers and candles, remained. I hated candles; I never let them burn in the house for fear of a fire. Seeing them flicker near the bark made me nervous. I did my best to ignore them and slipped into bed next to Janice. Her body was cold. I held my breath for a moment, terrified that she had slipped away without me noticing. I put my head on her chest and heard her heartbeat—slow, irregular, but it was beating. I kissed her on the face a few times and rolled over, hoping that tonight I would get a good night sleep, that tomorrow would be normal.

My mind swirled with countless thoughts and images. I tossed and turned, yet sleep still came. Around one in the morning I awoke to go to the bathroom. I wasn't surprised; my old bladder never let me sleep a full night anymore. After relieving myself, I shuffled back to bed, but I paused and looked at the clock. In thirty minutes, twenty-four hours would have passed since my nightmare began. I felt compelled to look outside at the tree. Looking out the window, I was surprised and a bit scared to see someone on my front lawn. If it was any other day and I saw a stranger in my lawn, I would panic, but tonight was different. I had to squint, but I could tell it was the father I had seen earlier that day. He was sitting with his back against the tree. In his hands was a beat-up old stuffed animal.

Guilt washed over me, for watching this man's private pain, for not saving his daughter. I wanted to talk to him, to comfort him, but I knew for a fact there was nothing in the world I could do that would help this man. No matter how many times people brought over casseroles or flowers for Janice, it did nothing but annoy me. Usually, I ended up having to comfort them, and doing so took time away from Janice. I shut the shade and went back to bed. The mirror attracted my gaze. The curtain was in clear view, and I knew that behind it was a man in pain.

It took almost an hour, but I had finally started to fall asleep again when I heard the noise. At first I thought the garbage disposal had turned on, that someone had jammed a dozen forks into it. As I sat up, the noise got louder. It wasn't in the house, but was outside. I looked at the clock; it was a bit after two. Not again. I couldn't handle something else happening. The temptation to lie back down and put the pillow over my head was overwhelming. As the noise grew louder, the pitch changed, and I knew instantly what it was: a chainsaw. With two quick steps, I was at the window. I pulled up the entire shade without hesitation or worry about disturbing his grief. Sure enough, there was the father, squinting hard as wood splinters shot past his face. The blade of the saw was already halfway through the trunk. I opened the window and screamed out of it as loudly as I could. It was useless—the roar of the engine and the tearing wood covered even my loudest scream. I had to go outside.

Three steps from the bedroom door, I realized Janice was awake. I turned to her and we locked eyes. For some reason, she mouthed *I love you* to me. I smiled and ran out the door. There were times when the pain

15

medication made her thoughts and speech unclear. I was sure this was one of them, because if she knew was going on, she wouldn't be saying that. Once my robe was on, I threw on a pair of sneakers, thinking of all the glass, and ran outside. To my horror, I saw the blade just about to break through the other side of the tree. Even if I stopped him at that second, the tree would still fall. It didn't stop me from trying. Running to him, waving my arms like a madman, I tried to get his attention. By the time I reached him, the tree was falling. The falling part didn't occur to me; it didn't seem to occur to the man, either, as the expression on his face turned to shock as the tree tipped towards my house and right towards the bedroom where Janice lay.

As the tree started to fall, I tried to stop my run and fell myself. Just as my body slammed into the ground, the top of the tree crashed through my roof. I could feel cuts on my elbows, and my left arm ached as if it were broken. As I looked at the house, the shingles sliding off, pieces of wood hanging loose, I wanted to throw up. Losing Janice was inevitable, but it wasn't supposed to be this way. Ignoring the pain and the man's hand on my shoulder, I got up. With my good arm, I pushed the sobbing, apologetic man off me and hobbled to the front door.

Inside the main entrance, there was no damage, though I wasn't relieved. As I turned the corner to go down the hall I saw the man follow me into the house. He was yelling something about a phone, but I ignored him. The ceiling in the hall was broken through, part of a branch where the light used to be. My feet crunched as I stepped on the pieces of ceiling and broken light fixture.

Our bedroom doorframe was still intact, which I took as good sign, even though it wasn't. The room was hardly recognizable. All I could see were leaves, branches, and shards of Janice's and my past life. Branch after branch I snapped with my bare hands as I tried to make my way to the bed. I was bleeding, shaking, and exhausted by the time I saw the corner of the bed.

There was a small clearing next to bed on the floor. I dropped to my knees and shuffled along the floor. Janice's hand was hanging off the side of the bed. I put my face to it and was surprised to find it warm. I took a deep breath, trying to get the courage to assess the state of Janice's body. Ready as I was ever going to be, I lifted my head. She wasn't dead. Janice was looking right in my direction, her face more alive than I'd seen it in months. She smiled and just stared at me. I didn't want to take my eyes off her face, but I had to check the damage. When I did, I let out a sob. A branch, a small one, had pierced Janice's chest. Other than that, there seemed to no more damage. I went to reach for the branch, but she put up her hand to stop me. Blood was pooling around the wound, staining her white nightgown red. I ripped the nightgown away to see how bad it was. The branch was deep, but I couldn't tell how deep. I didn't know what to do. Instinct made me want to rip it out, but I knew she would bleed to death if I did. Instead, I reached up and carefully snapped the branch off at the base so I could move her.

The broken branch started to ooze sap. The golden liquid ran down the branch in slow motion towards Janice's chest. All I could think about was infection. I grabbed a piece of sheet to wipe it away, but she again stopped me. I could hear the sirens in the background as the sap slowly ran down and into her wound. I couldn't help but think of the tears she had given to the tree all those years ago. Over and over again, I kissed Janice's hand until I was pulled away by a firefighter. Getting her into the ambulance, the ride, and the emergency room were all a blur. The next thing I knew, I was slumped over in a private waiting room, staring at my cell, not wanting to call my children.

When Janice first got the news of her tumor, I sat the girls down over ice cream. We were outside at a picnic table. The girls could tell something was wrong because I hadn't taken them out for cones since they were teens. When I told them their mother was going to die, that it was inevitable, they both came and sat beside me. I wrapped my arms around them and we cried as our ice cream melted. They felt good in my arms, my daughters, like they were kids again. Yet, at the same time, I never wanted to experience that again, their pain.

Mentally, I had prepared myself for Janice's death. The kids, on the other hand, refused to think she could die. According to them, some miracle cure would be found and she'd be saved. All I could think while I stared at that phone was that I was going to have to see my daughters cry again. When I heard the doctor's shoes clicking down the hall, I prepared myself for the news. I stood up, took a deep breath, and told myself I'd take it like a man. I'd known Dr. Damon for a while now; she was the one treating Janice. Yet, in all that time, I had never seen her smile like she was now. When she saw me, she hugged me and laughed hysterically. I wanted to push her away and scream. I thought she was laughing at how Janice died. *Miracle, Miracle, Miracle, Miracle.* The word rang in my head as Dr. Damon went on to explain how, against astronomical odds, the branch had pierced the tumor, pushing it away from the heart, making it operable. During the emergency surgery, they had removed the tumor. Other than the wound in her chest, she had no other problems. In fact, she was better than she had been in months. Janice could breathe with ease and her heart was beating steadily. She was going to be fine...fine. There was one thing, though—a tiny part of the branch was stuck inside of her. They couldn't remove it, but she could live just fine with it inside her, forever. The only word I heard was *live*.

Three months later, after church, Janice and I took a cutting of the White Ash tree and planted it where the old one used to be. Again, it took a lot of sweat and tears to get the tree to grow, but Janice got it to live—just like the tree had done for her.

THE EMPTY STOCKING

He hummed "Jingle Bells" to himself as he got the living room ready for Christmas morning. It had been a lot of work, like always, getting ready for the big day. The shopping, wrapping, and baking were exhausting, especially since he didn't have any help doing it this year. At least work had let him take a week off. He spent his free days shopping and used the nights to wrap presents and make homemade candy canes and gingerbread men. He even took one entire day to make the gingerbread house. Without the rest of his family it was a bit hard to hold the walls and put the roof on, but he managed.

He was pleasantly surprised at how good the candy cane he put in his mouth tasted. Carol had always made them. He had never done much but annoy her while she melted the sugar and rolled out the strips, always trying to grab one before they were done. He was proud of himself for making them so well. Carol would be stunned.

He checked his watch. It was just about eleven. Time for a break.

He plopped down on the couch and admired the tree. It was perfect. It took him four hours and three Christmas tree farms to find the perfect one. He cut it down himself, shook off the needles, and brought it home.

Carol loved white lights on the tree, but ever since Jimmy and Rachel could talk, they always wanted colorful, blinking lights. He did the colorful lights again this year. Besides, Carol enjoyed watching their happy kids more than a white tree. The tree was so beautiful. Every ball was in the perfect place, his homemade candy canes hanging from the fresh branches. He forced back a few tears, distracting himself with the presents under it. There were so many.

Like always, he had spoiled the kids. Probably twenty, thirty presents each. They deserved them. As for Carol, she didn't have as many, but they certainly cost as much. The diamond bracelet she always wanted (but he was too cheap to buy) was wrapped in shiny, red paper, along with every one of her favorite things: truffles, chocolate-coated cherries, bath beads. He was positive he hadn't missed a thing. Even the stockings were crammed full with candies and silly little toys the kids would love, even some joke gifts for Carol (that were marked with an X so she wouldn't open them in front of the kids). As his gaze went over the mantel, he admired the stockings. His mother had made them for the whole family a few years back and even stitched their names in the tops. Everyone loved them; they were so much bigger than typical stockings. Fingering the gentle lettering on Carol's, he realized his was empty; not a single thing inside, it hung flat as a board.

He hadn't bought himself anything; then again, why would he? For one, he didn't deserve any presents. A tiny bit of panic started to wash over him, for everything wasn't perfect with a stocking empty. He looked at his watch again. Less than an hour before Christmas.

21

Nothing would be open now. He raced to the bedroom, pulled open a drawer, and grabbed a handful of socks. It might be cheating, but at least the stocking looked full. That made him feel a bit better.

With one last check, he was satisfied. Everything was ready. Just three more things to do. First, he turned on the television, to the channel that played the burning fireplace and Christmas music for twenty-four hours. He kept the volume on low, but loud enough to hear it. The kids always got a kick out of the fake fire. And what was opening presents without the music? Staring at the fire, he let one tear fall. Why not? Christmas was almost here.

In the kitchen, he carefully arranged a plate of the gingerbread men, poured a large glass of milk, and got another small plate of carrots. He remembered last year when the kids ran to the living room, saw the presents, and screamed. When they saw the cookies half-eaten and the carrots nibbled, they totally freaked out, ran to Carol and him and dragged them to the plate to show them. Jimmy was especially fascinated. He held up the carrot, touched the nibble marks, and said, *I think Rudolph ate this one.* He would have gone on to say which reindeer ate which carrot but, not wanting to wait any longer to open presents, Rachel pulled him away.

Shaking off the cold shiver that ran down his back, down his legs to his feet, he marched the cookie plate into the living room and placed it by the fireplace. A few years ago, he had tried to put the plate for Santa on the end table, but Rachel was so worried Santa wouldn't see it that she wouldn't go to bed until he moved it by the fire. Since then, he had placed it in the same place each year. Kneeling down in front of the fireplace, he picked up one carrot at a time, nibbled off half, making darn sure they looked like an animal had done it, and put them back. The carrots were perfect. He even took bigger nibbles on one. That way, Jimmy would find one that stood out and say his favorite reindeer ate it. Then, it was on to the cookies. He ate two whole cookies and half of a third, making sure that a good number of crumbs fell on the plate. Downing half the glass of milk, he took some crumbs from the cookies, put them on his lip, and pushed them against the rim. Authenticity counted when it came to kids. Setting the nibbled food and glass back down, he laughed. It was his best work yet!

Taking one more look around, he took all the Christmas joy in, and reached for the golden knob to the fireplace that was only a few inches behind the milk, turning it all the way on. The gas rushed out in a loud hiss. The sound annoyed him a bit, so he turned up the music on the television. Ironically, or more so fittingly, "Blue Christmas" was playing. Shaking his head, he grabbed the Santa hat he wore every Christmas morning while the kids opened presents and put it on. The soft lining always felt so good on his forehead. After adjusting two more ornaments so they were perfect, he took a seat on the couch.

The smell of gas was starting to fill his nose. It stung a bit, but he did his best to ignore it. All he had to do was fall asleep. When he woke up, Carol would be sitting next to him, holding his hands and smiling so big, so big it would look as if it hurt. They would kiss lightly and she would whisper *Merry Christmas* in his ear. Then, before he could sneak another kiss, the kids would run into the room, scream their heads off, and he would grab

23

them, kiss their necks and heads, tell them he loved them, just like he should have before they…

He missed those kisses, missed Carol, missed them all so much. Christmas was always their day and theirs only. When he woke up, they would have the best Christmas ever—and he would never be without them again.

WAKE UP STRONG

The Husband

Whatever happened to our inner glow? The joy that used to radiate out of us. Show on our faces, gleam in our eyes, and dance on our lips? Instead, our eyes are now dead, bored, and glazed over as we sit and watch the television instead of looking at each other. Our lips, they are silent. Only grunts about work and the latest *CSI* episode slip out from them. We sit together, eat together, watch TV together, sleep next to each other—yet, we hardly even know we exist.

You kiss me goodbye in the morning, but it's routine, not love. We call to check in with one another during the day, but is it out of responsibility or because we actually want to hear one another's voices? The only things we do together are watch movies and television, things that involve little or no conversation. And when we do talk, it's always one-sided—I yap away, and you listen and nod as a mother would to child who goes on and on about a new cartoon.

We give each other the obligatory kiss goodnight; though our lips touch, our tongues dance only once every few weeks. In a matter of seconds, you are sound asleep, leaving me alone to stare at the ceiling and think about how I'm losing you more every day. Some nights, I lie there for hours thinking of how I want to be in love with you, wondering why I'm not anymore and what I could do to get it back. We are still young; we shouldn't be in this position until we have been married twenty years. Even then, I always hoped that I would still melt when I saw my wife, that I would still want to sweep her up in my arms, kiss her, and love her with all I had. And, yet, here we are. Two zombies to the world. Wake up, work, eat, TV, sleep, and repeat.

As I finally start to drift away each night, I pledge to myself that I will wake up strong. That I will have the strength to love you again, to give myself completely to you. But I never do. There are times when I do wake up feeling confident, but it is usually only a matter of minutes until my efforts are crushed. Usually by something so small, so insignificant that it makes me sick that I crumble and give up because of it. Something as small as you not looking at me when you kiss me goodbye—that tiny piece can make me
give up for days.

Then there are the days when I do make it a bit longer. I try, you try; they are decent days, but they forced, awkward, and not real. They seem to be getting less and less frequent as well. We used to have good months, then weeks. Now we are sliding past good days; hours are next. I don't even want to think what happens when those pass as well.

Maybe if I was normal, this wouldn't bother me. Normal as in, if I was content just to have a companion to live life with, someone to be there for me—because you are, but that is not enough for me. I need more. I need the attention you once gave me. I need the love that once poured from you with no end in sight. For years, we talked for hours on the phone every night without fail; now, now we hardly exchange words at night, for that would interrupt our shows.

I don't even want to discuss sex. Yes, we have it once every other week, but there is no passion, no love. It's merely a task to relieve the pressure of not having it. A task almost like having to release the pressure in a boiler so it doesn't blow. We do it because we have to, not because we want to. What happened to when we used to spend all day in bed, trying to beat our record for number of times in a day? I was always so determined to please you more times than you could handle. We would hold each other and squeeze tighter with every thrust because we couldn't get close enough to each other. Now, now our bodies hardly touch; we finish and mumble that it was good before sliding off and cleaning up instead of holding each other and kissing, not caring about the mess.

Our anniversary is in less than a month. If things don't change by then, if I can't finally convince myself to wake up strong and stay that way, then I'll have…something will have to change. For I can't fall asleep another night with these thoughts trapped in my head.

The Wife

What is it that keeps you up every night? Your tossing and turning wakes me up time and again, but I ignore it. Why do I do that? Why am I scared to ask him what is wrong? Maybe it's the truth that I'm scared of? Is he cheating on me? Is that why we are slipping away from what we used to be? I mean, things are fine, they're nice, we have a routine. I like that. But I need more attention and he just doesn't give it to me.

Of course, I could probably give him more, but he just doesn't seem to want it. Maybe work is keeping him stressed out. Whatever it is, I'm sure it'll pass. We'll get over this hump. Besides, when I tell him that I'm pregnant, that will bring his real emotions out, make him love me more than I can love him back. We'll finally be able to go back to the way we were, being happy and in love. It'll be wonderful. So why am I waiting to tell him?

THE PRIEST AND THE PLANE

Jack was an atheist; the priest was not.

It was to be a forty-minute plane ride, the last leg in Jack's usual flight home for the weekend. He was sick of this flight. Two layovers, five hours total, twice a week. Being a consultant wasn't bad, but having to be away from home and his wife was torture. The flights on Monday mornings were the worst. He had to get up at four a.m. to make check-in. He hated getting up that early, saying goodbye to Mary, knowing he wasn't going to see her until ten on Friday night. He had to keep telling himself that it was going to get him a promotion, that he'd be able to get a position where he wouldn't have to fly so much. That he'd be stationed at home before Mary got pregnant with their first child.

The flights home weren't as bad. They still were annoying, tiny planes with uncomfortable seats and passengers with bad breath, gas, or both. The only good part was that he could get work done, work he wouldn't have to do on the weekend. The best part of the flights was the smiling. He couldn't help but smile, for he knew in a few hours he'd be having a Friday night lovemaking session and sleeping late on Saturday, which he would

29

spend lounging around with Mary. Yes, the Friday flights were tolerable.

This particular Friday he hoped, like he always did, that no one would be sitting next to him. The plane was always tiny, so small he had to bend his six-foot-two frame in half to walk down the aisle. The seats were no better. With someone next to him, it was misery. It was why he always picked an aisle seat. At least, that way, he could stretch his legs into the aisle and get some room. The inside seats were unbearable.

Ducking into the doorway, the usual flight attendant, Maggie, greeted him with a playful smile that he returned with a wink. She flirted with him often, but he always ignored it.

Halfway down the aisle, his eyes locked on his seat with relief. Seat 11B, his usual, and thankfully no one was sitting in the seat next to it—yet. He took off his tie and coat, rolled them up, and placed them in the tiny bin above his seat. Then, he put his briefcase under the seat in front of him like a good passenger. He rubbed his eyes and tried to relax and turn his mind over to weekend mode before attacking the few files he had to review before he could actually enjoy the weekend. As he rubbed his eyes, he said a mantra over and over, as he always did when the seat next to him was empty: *Please, oh God, please let there be no one next to me.* It was always a tense ten-minute wait to see if that wish would come true. And, if it did, he knew his weekend would be even better.

Five minutes passed. He was relaxing a bit more and feeling pretty good about having both seats to himself. The plane was rather full, like it always was on Friday, and no passengers had come on in the last few minutes. Jack felt excited; he knew they would be shutting the door soon. Then, in the blink of an eye, a man appeared. A priest. Gray-haired, small, in full garb with no carry-on, but a big dark bible. He looked a bit stressed walking down the aisle. There were three other empty seats and Jack prayed that the man would sit in each one as he passed. The priest's eyes saw the empty seat next to Jack and lit up with relief.

This was not going to be a good flight.

Jack would have been annoyed with anyone coming to sit next to him. But a priest? That infuriated him. Not that he had anything against religion or priests. He was an atheist, a proud one at that, but he still avoided conversations about religion at all costs. He had learned to do that quickly in life. When someone finds out you're an atheist, they look at you differently. As if you are a serial killer or a monster just because you don't believe in what they do. If an average person gets offended, he could only imagine what a priest would think.

"Excuse me, I believe that is my seat, next to yours," the priest said to Jack with almost no smile, as if he, too, were dreading sitting next to someone. Jack got up with a forced smile, let the small man settle in, and sat back down, trying not to sigh too loudly. He only hoped that the man would not be chatty and would keep to himself. After buckling his seatbelt, Jack pulled out a file and began to read, mostly to look busy.

For the first five minutes, the priest was silent, except for a few deep sighs to himself as he settled. The flight attendant went through her spiel and the plane began to taxi. Jack prayed to himself, hoping the priest would stay silent. No such luck.

"Would you like to pray with me before takeoff? A blessing for the road?" the priest asked in a chipper voice. Jack swallowed hard, contemplating blurting out he was an atheist or lying and going along with him. He cleared his throat a few times to buy time, then finally chose a third option.

"No. Thanks, though." Jack didn't look to see the priest's reaction. He did hear his mumbled prayer and the kisses he gave the rosary and bible.

The plane took off and, for ten minutes, there was nothing but the hum of the engines, clicks on keyboards, and the shuffling of papers as the mostly business-oriented passengers occupied their time. It was when the drinks came around that things changed. Maggie brought Jack a Bloody Mary, his usual drink, without asking, then asked the priest what he would like. Scotch. Jack had to stop himself from looking at the man with curiosity. It didn't matter, though—the priest could tell he was surprised.

"What? Think a man of the cloth isn't allowed a drink every now and then?" he asked with a laugh, obviously trying to incite the same from Jack. Jack forced himself to look at the man and smile, but didn't respond and went back to his papers, hoping to end the conversation there.

"My name is Father Murry."

Suddenly, there was a hand in front of Jack, and he had no choice but to take it. "Jack. Nice to meet you." Again, he went back to his papers, trying to avoid the inevitable conversation.

"I'm guessing you take this flight often. The lady brought you a drink without even asking."

Still avoiding looking at him, acting busy, Jack responded, "Yeah, every week."

"Ah, well, this is the only time I'll be taking this flight. First and last really." Jack was intrigued, but didn't ask. He just smiled again.

"Retiring to a new church. I worked in a big city for years. Looking forward to being in a small community to live out the last of my days." Jack could feel the man's eyes boring into him as he took a sip of his drink. He wanted to tell the man he had work to do, that he was busy and sorry, but for some reason he just couldn't bring himself to be rude.

"That's nice." Jack said hoping that keeping his eyes on his work would make the point that he wanted to be left alone.

"You know, work isn't everything in life." Father Murry said, reaching over and tapping Jack's file hard in the middle of the page.

The invasion of his personal space, the boldness of touching his property, infuriated Jack. Again, if this weren't a priest, he would give him a snide remark. Instead, he responded as kindly as he could. "Yeah, but when you need to eat, live in a house, and wear clothing it's sort of inevitable, don't you think? Not all of us have jobs that provide all that." Finishing the sentence, he regretted it. There was a long pause. Jack was about to apologize when the man's hand once again entered his space. This time, it grabbed the folder out of his hands, closed it, and stuffed it in the chair back. Jack's mouth dropped open; he was amazed that the man had the balls

33

to do such a thing. Finally, he turned and looked the priest in the eyes. The man held his gaze, didn't back down. It wasn't until Jack looked away that the priest spoke again.

"I was you once." The priest said it and let the words hang in the air. Jack looked around, wishing other people would start to chat so that this conversation wouldn't be the only one echoing around the cabin.

"And what does that mean?" Jack asked snidely, once again avoiding eye contact.

"I was just like you. I had a high-powered job in an insurance company. I was twenty-six and on the track to run the company before I was thirty. I was making six figures—over forty years ago. Nothing mattered to me. Nothing but the job, the money, the promotions. It consumed me. I forgot that the world even existed outside of my job. I'd stay late, bring work home, work weekends. All to make more money. Money I didn't even spend because I worked too much. I was too busy to even ask the woman I loved to marry me. She left and I worked more." The priest paused to sip his scotch. Jack had downed his drink during the man's monologue and was trying to get Maggie's attention to get another.

"A year later, I got sick. It wasn't anything terminal, yet I almost died, because I ignored the symptoms for so long. I couldn't take a day off of work! Hell no! Instead, I let a cold turn into pneumonia, which got so bad I ended up in the hospital after collapsing at my desk while working late. No one found me until the next day. A few hours more, and I would have died. I spent the next three weeks in the hospital fighting for my life." His words were getting louder; more emotion spilled into each sentence, making Jack feel more and more uncomfortable.

Maggie finally came over with another drink for Jack. The priest asked for another as well, and she went to retrieve it. He took a few long sighs and waited for the drink to come. When it did, he took a sip and began to speak, but Jack cut him off.

"I'm sorry, but why are you telling me all of this? Is this a speech you usually give to the person sitting next to you on a plane?" Jack demanded, looking at the man's hands instead of his face. He watched the priest pour the tiny bottle's contents over the chunks of ice in his glass. Again, he felt stupid. He couldn't even figure out why he was being so rude. The only reason he could think of was how
uncomfortable he felt next to this man.

"Truthfully, this is my first flight in thirty-six years. So, no. I don't tell everyone I sit next to. I may have used it in a sermon a few times, but that is a bit different."

"So, why are you telling me? Is church in session right now or something?" Again, Jack felt his gut tighten as he heard his own words. The priest chuckled a bit.

"Let me guess, you're not religious?"

Jack responded by shaking his head.

"Agnostic or atheist?" the priest asked, a bit too loudly for Jack's taste.

Jack tried to answer, but his throat had gone dry. No one ever asked him this straight out—certainly never a priest. He finished his second drink in two gulps and decided to answer truthfully, not to lie. His beliefs were just that, *his* beliefs.

35

"Atheist..." It was almost a whisper. When he finished saying it, he looked around and made sure no one was looking at him. And, though no one was, he could tell they were listening, all of them.

"I respect that. I do, really. Unlike some preachers, I understand atheists. I mean, at times, I find it's hard myself."

Jack kept listening without looking at the man and got Maggie's attention once again for another drink. She made a face at him to show her surprise.

"Would you look at me, kid? Would you have a conversation with me like you would with your business partners? Just because I work for someone you don't believe in doesn't mean I don't deserve the respect of a human being."

Jack sighed, taking his drink from Maggie, who tried in vain to start a conversation. He took a sip, then looked at the priest. "I'm sorry. It's just—I get nervous being, well, an atheist. With you sitting here, I panicked. I didn't mean to be rude."

The priest smiled big and patted Jack on the shoulder. Jack couldn't help but crack a smile as well.

The pilot made an announcement about upcoming turbulence just as the plane dipped down and back up hard. That finally got a few grumbles from the rest of the passengers, and a few even chatted for a second. The priest and Jack ignored it.

"So, Jack, I know it is probably scary to talk about this with a priest, but, may I ask why you're an atheist?"

Jack took a big sigh and steadied his drink from the plane's bumping and jiving. Delaying his answer, he swirled the drink a bit.

"Well, just a lot of stuff, really. Hard childhood, one that no kid should have. Then, not to be rude, but education. I questioned things, starting researching, and just came to a logical—well, logical to me—conclusion." Jack looked at the priest, whose big smile put him at ease, oddly enough.

"I mean, there are over 200 religions in the world. Who is to say which one is right? You know? Like, no offense, but why is yours more real than someone who worships rats?"

"It's not. Not at all. A religion is what it means to that person."

Jack thought of the priest's response for a second and turned to him. "So you're saying that a religion that worships rats is just as important as yours?"

The priest smiled and chuckled a bit. "Well, I think worshipping rats is a bit creepy, but what I'm trying to say, Jack, is that there may be all sorts of religions, but they were created by one entity. Just because different cultures interpreted it differently doesn't mean they are wrong. God is a mysterious man—he's just happy that people believe in something. Even if it's rats or ten different gods, in the end they are all praying to him."

"I must say you are the most open-minded religious person I have ever talked to. So many are like, *Our religion is right, everything else is wrong!* I mean, think of all the wars started by religion—heck almost all have been."

"And those are the ones who are getting it wrong." Jack listened to those words and instantly liked this man. He shared Jack's views, yet they were completely opposite. The two smiled at each other, then grimaced as the plane took another sharp bump. The pilot came on and apologized, but said it was only going to get worse and asked that the flight attendant stay seated.

The priest patted Jack's shoulder, looked into his eyes, and spoke. "Don't worry, God is watching out for me! And with you sitting so close to me, I guess that means you're safe, too!" he said with a hearty laugh. Jack joined the laugh. For a few minutes, there was an awkward silence between them as they both realized the plane situation was a bit scarier than they would have liked.

The plane dipped hard, shot to the right, and went on a fast descent for a full five seconds before pulling back up and steadying. The cabin echoed with cries of worry. The priest laughed. Jack just thought of his wife and the promotion this plane ride was going to someday get him.

"Guess now is a good time to reconsider your beliefs!" The priest laughed hard. Jack smiled, but started to wonder about the man. He was the only cool-headed person there. The only one not panicking.

"I'm just teasing you, boy. You'll be fine. But if it does slow up, I would love to continue our conversation. I think it would only get more interesting. Don't worry, I won't try to convert you. Those people who make that their lives' work, they aren't doing God's work—they just enjoy making people follow their beliefs. People need to come to faith on their own, not from pressure."

"I'll tell you, I was dreading sitting next to you, but you know what..." Before Jack could finish his sentence, the plane did a corkscrew, turning upside-down and starting to head straight toward earth. Items flew about the cabin, laptops knocked into heads, drinks stained everything, and almost everyone screamed. Heading toward the earth, Jack forgot completely about the priest until he noticed a hand holding his. Someone from another row yelled, "Father, pray for us!" Having a hard time keeping from throwing up, Jack looked to the priest, who gave him a wink, then went about praying to himself and kissing the bible in his hand.

When Jack woke up, he had forgotten he was in a plane, let alone a crash. For a few seconds, he thought he was hung over and tried to remember what he had done the night before. Then the sobbing, the smell of melted plastic and burning flesh, forced his eyes open to the horror all around him. He was still holding the priest's hand, and looked over to ask if he was alright. He was not. A large chunk of metal was lodged in the priest's forehead, holding his body up in a sitting position. Blood trickled down the steel and dripped onto the bible he was still clutching in his hand. In disbelief, Jack turned his attention to himself. There was no blood on him, no cuts, no scratches, nothing he could find. He felt fine except for a headache.

Looking around, he saw that the front of the plane was gone, crushed inward, turning the pilots, Maggie, and the first three rows of passengers into a mash of human meat and metal. Everyone else seemed to be alive, as most of them were moving. He tried his seatbelt, which unlatched with ease. As he was about to sit up, he felt a hand tug at him. He couldn't believe the priest was still alive. Turning, he saw the priest hadn't moved, not an inch. When he looked down at the priest's hands, the bible seemed to scream at him. It didn't move nothing had changed about it except for the ever-darkening pages being soaked with blood. He knew he had to take it. Pulling it from the man's fingers, he shook off some of the blood, stood, and tucked the book into his waistline.

Jack instantly headed for the back exit, yet as he twisted the handle and pushed the door out, he didn't go through it. He looked around, saw that there was grass and that it was safe to exit, and headed back into the cabin. As he walked back up the aisle, hands grabbed at him, cries of agony and for help rang out—then, someone called for him.

"Father! Help me Father!" cried a bleeding man. Jack wanted to say he wasn't the priest, but thought it was a waste of time. Instead, he went about finding a sharp enough piece of steel to cut the seatbelt off the old man. Once free, the man stood up and said, "Thank you, Father, thank you," and exited the plane. Jack worked his way up to the front of the plane. At the mash of steel in the front, there were only two passengers still alive. One, a woman bleeding from the forehead, also called him Father. He freed her and looked at the unconscious teenager in the next seat. Jack placed his hands on his face. The boy snapped awake, coughed, smiled, and called him Father as Jack freed him.

The same thing happened, passenger after passenger as Jack cut their seatbelts, helped them up, and let them out. They all thanked him, called him Father. All the ones that were unconscious awoke at his touch and left the plane safely. When everyone was gone, Jack returned to free the priest's body in case the plane kept burning, yet he couldn't find him. He checked the seat number. He had the right one, but he was gone. The piece of steel was there; it hadn't moved and was still covered in blood. Jack figured someone else must have taken the body off the plane. Seeing no one else to help, he left the plane. When got outside, his life changed forever.

Two years later, Jack hadn't talked about the event. Not with anyone. Not the news crews that wouldn't leave him alone for months about the "miracle flight." Not even with his wife, who was hurt that he wouldn't open up. It wasn't until his first child, Murry, was in his crib on the first day home and his wife was resting that he told the story. The whole story. He told Murry every detail, explained how he didn't believe in God, that he still wasn't sure he existed. He still wasn't even sure after reading the bible four times. He told his son how Father Murry's body had disappeared from the plane, how they had only found his blood. Some reports said he must have burnt up. Others claimed it was a miracle. He told his son about how he researched the priest for months, finding out everything he could, which wasn't much. He told his child how he couldn't explain what happened. That when he walked out of the plane and saw all the passengers kneeling in a semi-circle, holding hands, that he had cried and walked into the middle of them. He went on to tell Murry about how they had all looked at him like he was a savior. That they continued to call him Father and, to this day, send him cards and letters. Lastly, he told Murry that when he grew up, he would get the bloodstained bible.

PEBBLES

Tiny, big. Sharp, round. Jagged, smooth. Some pierced his flesh, hurting his face badly. Saliva and mucus mixed with some smaller ones, making a small pool of mud. He didn't care and he didn't notice. Nothing mattered. Not the pain in his face, nor the filth on his clothing. The only thing of any importance was the one thing he couldn't do anything about.

It was a day that Chase had planned for over six months, making sure every single aspect would be perfect. He hoped that Molly hadn't been suspicious of his plans, even though he'd asked her to take the hike a week-and-a-half ahead of time (when they usually made plans the day before). They had been camping and backpacking at least a dozen times throughout their relationship, which would be two years on Thursday.

Their journey that day was to hike up a new mountain (new for Molly, at least). Chase always said it was no fun if you knew your way up it. "What's the point of doing something you've already accomplished?" That was the excuse he only had to give to Molly once. From that point on, they always hiked different mountains— though they were usually in the same mountain range.

Having the day off from work put them both in a good mood the morning they left. Getting away from the hustle and bustle of their daily lives and the busy little city was always a relief. Of course, they hit Maggie's, their favorite breakfast place, to fill up their guts with energy-filled, fattening foods, a tradition before every hike. After that, it was on the road, with no planned stops; they had everything they needed and could usually make the ride, which lasted a few hours, without having to go the bathroom.

Usually, their method for picking a mountain was simple: drive up into the range until you found one that looked fun and not too hard, park, and hike. When they first started, they had used national parks with trails, but quickly found them to be too populated and too easy. Going off the beaten path on ground that no one had probably walked in hundreds of years—now *that* was an adventure!

When they reached the mountain range, Molly sat up in the car to put on her shoes. Any time they drove more than an hour, she took them off—a quirk Chase loved.

"Oh, how about that one over there?" Molly pointed to a range to the left while putting her straight, sandy-colored hair behind her ear in the process, another constant habit. Chase shrugged and kept driving. They repeated this several times until Chase, doing his best to pretend he was seeing the mountain for the first time, spoke up.

"Hey, look at this road here. I bet if we go down it, we could park and go up that one?"

Molly gave him a suspicious look, leaned forward to look up at the mountain. "Don't you think that one is a bit...too big?"

"Nothing we couldn't conquer together," Chase replied with a smirk, suddenly trying to foreshadow his intentions.

The road was long and jagged, with countless holes to circumnavigate. It took them a while, but when they finally reached the end of it, they found a small parking area and the foundation of a long forgotten home. There were no other cars around, and when they got out of theirs, they heard the warming silence of nature. Pure sounds. Not polluted by people and machines, just animals and Mother Nature. They both didn't speak for several minutes so as not to spoil the serenity of it. Eventually, Chase laughed as he tripped on part of the foundation they were exploring.

"Must have been an old cabin. Looks as if it burnt down or fell apart a hundred years ago," Chase said, using his best *CSI* tone as he examined some old, crumbling materials on the ground.

"Yeah, but hikers must come here a lot. That road isn't overgrown yet."

"True, but at least it is just us today!" With that, he scooped her up and gave her a sweet kiss. They had both acknowledged their anniversary that morning with a quick, passionate tumble in bed. And when they got back from their hike, they were supposed to shower and go to a fancy meal at the restaurant where they'd had their first date. It was all going to be so perfect.

They started on a small path by the back of the foundation. It was thin and hardly used. They followed it to a stream, and then it seemed to disappear. This was the part they usually loved. Checking the compass, making note of their direction and the placement of the sun, they headed into uncharted territory. Only this time, Chase knew exactly where he was going. His one hiker friend told him of a peak with a clearing perfect for a picnic and a view that stretched for miles. Last week, he had taken a day off work, followed the map his friend made him, and lost his breath when he reached the clearing. It was exactly what he was looking for. On the way down, he had made darn sure to remember how to get back to it, and even put some marks in trees to keep him on course without having to use the map. After making the hike once again last night at sunset, he knew finding his way would be no problem. The only hard part was making it look as if he was just hiking at random.

After the first hour of trudging up the steep incline, they sat down to drink from their bottles and eat oranges from their backpacks. Again, it was their typical routine. Depending on how steep the mountain was, they would stop anywhere from the first hour to two hours into the hike. With this one being so steep, they only made it an hour.

"This is a tough one!" Molly said between swigs.

"I'm sure it will be worth it, though," he said with too big of a smile. She had to be suspicious, but it didn't matter—it wouldn't ruin the surprise by any means.

"Alright, let's get going. I want to try to make it to the top before we head back." They had a strict rule of three hours up, max. After three hours, they would stop their climb, rest, and head back down. Sometimes they finished the mountain, but usually they didn't. This was

45

Chase's rule. His theory was that if they reached the mountain by ten, started up for three hours, and headed back, it would take them two more hours to get back down, putting them at the car by three. This left room for emergencies. But the main reason for it was to never, ever get stuck on the mountain in the dark. When he was a child, he and his father once hiked too long and got stuck on the mountain with no sleep gear or food. It got so dark that they could hardly see in front of them and, because it was the dry season, they couldn't start a fire. They ended up spending the night hugging on the ground, cold and starving. Chase was sure to never let that happen again.

The hike up was long and hard, filled with many water breaks. It was a rather warm day, making it all the more difficult—though, the higher they got, the cooler it became. Chase couldn't help but smile as he thought about the moment that lay ahead of them. His grin was so big he did his best to keep in front of Molly so she wouldn't see it. On top of his excitement he was also a bit nervous; it was a big step, after all. It was those nerves that kept him from talking much, something he knew Molly would find suspicious.

"This hike is really going to make us hungry for dinner!" he said in a shaky voice that was not his usual. He winced at himself as he said it, knowing he probably sounded like a teenager on a first date trying to make conversation.

"Uh…yeah…" Molly said in a curious manor. Another hour later and Chase knew they were only a few minutes away; he saw the peak in the distance and the small path that led around the jagged rock. It was a tiny path that filled a normal person with fear as the ledge to the left dropped off a good seventy feet. It was so narrow you almost had to walk one foot in front of the other. It was creepy, but after about ten yards it came to a large clearing that he suspected was once used by natives as a lookout and smoke signal area. It was a perfect twenty-foot-round circle with only one way in and one way out— the skinny path. One could camp there with the best views in the world or have a romantic picnic...

"Looks like a path over there. Why don't we try that?" Again he tried to act normal, though now he was sweating more than usual. Arriving at the path, Chase stopped and turned to Molly.

"It looks really narrow. Why don't I take a quick look and make sure it's safe? Then I'll come back and get you." Molly agreed while taking a peek over the edge and making a face of fright. Chase disappeared around the path he had already navigated several times. He wasn't surprised at all when the waterproof bag he had placed there the night before was still there. With trembling hands, he quickly laid out a red checkered blanket, two champagne glasses, a bottle of Cristal (which had cost him a week's salary, but was going to be worth every penny), and a bowl of strawberries. He then dug into his pocket and checked the ring—it was still gorgeous. For the last month, he had taken it out an average of a dozen times a day to look at it, clean it, and imagine it on Molly's finger. Half the time, he would start to daydream and imagine kissing a wrinkled hand goodnight with that ring on it. He just couldn't wait to make her his wife.

"Chase? You alright?" Molly called from around the corner.

"Be right there!" Standing up, he checked the setup. Perfect. He turned to look over the cliff edge and at the view—it was splendid. He only hoped he could get through the proposal without crying. With a quick shuffle, he was back by Molly, who was staying as far from the edge as possible. She never liked being near the cliff edges, but he always talked her through the scarier ones they had to navigate. Just like now.

"Just follow me. Keep your eyes on the path. It's only a few yards, and then there is a clearing. It's nice." Their feet crunched on the loose gravel as they walked. When Chase rounded the edge, he quickly ran over to the blanket and took a standing position behind it. He watched as she came around the edge, her eyes glued to the ground. In the clearing, he could see her face relax a bit now that she was safe, but they quickly scrunched up again at the sight of the blanket and setup.

Chase watched as her face went from confusion, to shock, to excitement. He waited for her eyes to focus on him before he opened his mouth. As he started to speak, she covered her own mouth with both of her hands. He hoped it was a good sign.

"Molly. It's been two years now, a perfect two years." He could feel the tears start to choke up his throat.

"I can't imagine being without you. Hell, I hate just leaving you to go to work." He cleared his throat, fished for the small box in his pocket, took a step forward, and knelt down in front of the blanket and Molly.

"What I'm trying to say is that I want to spend the rest of my life with you." Opening the box, he felt tears come out of his eyes as he watched the tears build up in hers.

"Molly, will you marry me?" Finally, she dropped her hands from her face. Her mouth was wide open, her lips quivering. He pulled the ring out of the box and grasped her hand. With one gentle slide, he had the ring on her finger. She was turning red now and shaking.

"Oh, my God. Oh, my GOD!" she screamed in joy, slowly starting to move.

"Is that a yes, then?"

She smiled big, starting to jump up and down and move around frantically in her excitement. It was Chase who noticed that she had backed up to the edge.

"Molly, don't back up any more!" he screamed as he darted up from his kneeling position, reaching out towards her. But it was too late. Her left foot had already stepped back onto nothing. With her left hand out in front of her to look at the ring, she instantly started to fall backwards. Her arms swooped in huge circles as she tried to regain her balance, but gravity was already winning. Chase's fingers slapped the tips of hers as she fell backwards and disappeared from his view. With nothing for him to grab onto, to keep him from going over as well, he dropped to his stomach and reached for her, even though she was already twenty feet down. A split second later, she hit the jagged rock wall and rolled on her side, flipping over and over, again and again, until she hit a tree with her arm. It slowed her a bit and changed her direction, but she kept going, hitting three more trees until she came to an abrupt stop on top of two pine tree trunks that stuck straight out. Chase screamed her name, the words *no* and *help*, over and over again—to no avail.

49

There was a long pause while Chase held his breath and watched Molly, waiting for her to move. In his head, he begged her to move anything—flinch, twitch, *something* to show him she was still alive. Then, her neck moved from side to side, ever so slightly. That meant it wasn't broken; she could be alive!

"MOLLY!" It took six throat-ripping screams to get her to open her eyes. He watched as she looked around, trying to figure out where she was, then finally looked up at Chase. He could see her mouth move a bit, but he didn't know if she was talking or just trying to.

"Don't move, honey. Just—just stay still!" Chase screamed again, not sure what to tell her or even what to do. After a few seconds, he thought of his binoculars in the backpack and dove for them. With them in hand, he lay back down and focused them until he could see Molly clearly in the small viewfinder. He looked at her face first. His breath was sucked out of him when he saw that her nose was broken and bleeding. There was a gash on her forehead and, it was hard to tell, but her ear might have been totally torn off. Next, he carefully looked at her neck, which amazingly looked fine. Her arms were scraped raw and her right arm looked broken, but it was hard to tell with so many scrapes. Her pelvis was impossible to see under the clothing, but it didn't look as if any blood was seeping through. That was a good sign. It was her legs that horrified him. The left leg was bent entirely the wrong way and dangling below her as if it might just fall off. The other one was torn open, dripping blood at a rate so fast it made his stomach turn. If she didn't stop that bleeding, she wouldn't last long.

Getting up, Chase ran around the ledge, looking for any possible way down. On the far right there was a jagged rock wall. It looked almost climbable, but about ten feet down, it dropped. He could climb down and let go from there, but the fall would almost guarantee a broken leg for him. It wasn't an option. The rest of the ledge was the same way. It jutted out and then shot back in, making it impossible to climb down. There were several trees about ten feet away—he could try to jump then climb down, but if he missed them... Climbing down the mountain, then running around the base and back up to her, was the only possible way. But it would take him at least an hour or more to get down and another two to get back up to her. *If he could get back up.* She was stuck in the tree bases; below her was another fifty-foot drop. What if he couldn't make that climb up to her? Even if he did make it up to her, it would be impossible to get her down because he would have to carry her. After racing back and forth on the ledge, he stopped, grabbed his hair, and screamed.

It was then that he thought of the fire tower. If there were people up there, he could get their attention! With his binoculars, he found the old wooden tower in the distance and searched it for life. *Please, someone be on duty, please.* A coat, there was a coat! It was hanging on one of the studs. It only caught his eye because it blew a bit in the wind. Back and forth he swept the binoculars over the box. No one, no one? Unless they were lying down, no one was in there. The ladder. Maybe *they are on the ladder below.* Four times he passed the lenses over the ladders and close to the ground. Not a soul. Just in time, he caught himself from smashing the binoculars on the rocks—he might need them.

Dumping out his bag, he couldn't find one damn thing that might come in handy. The cell phones were in the car; they didn't work in the parking lot, let alone up here. On his knees, pebbles grinding into his skin, he cried. There was nothing he could do but leave her to get help. Which he didn't want to do, as he didn't think she would live that long. Falling to his stomach, he pulled himself to the ledge again. She looked more conscious this time, lifting her head. Her mouth was still moving. He tried as hard as he could to hear what she was saying, pointing his ear toward her, cupping a hand around it, but he could hear nothing but nature.

As his head hung over the edge, he cried, watching his tears fall and disappear from view on their way down to Molly. He loved that woman down there, more than he loved his own life, and he might have killed her. The guilt started to wash over him. It became harder and harder to breathe, as if the boulders above him had landed on his back. What the hell could he do? What should he do? In the distance, he could hear a helicopter purring its way over the landscape. Instantly, he thought of the tourist flights that flew low over the mountains to give the city folk an amazing view of nature. They used to piss him off so much that, every time they flew over, he would moon them. They advertised about seeing nature; flying over it, letting out exhaust fumes and an obnoxious amount of noise, was not seeing nature. It was ruining it. Though, right now, he couldn't have loved them more.

Jumping up, he flapped his arms, screamed, and jumped up and down as the helicopter approached. When it was about three hundred yards away, he saw it start to curve away from his direction. He had to do something that would get someone's attention, but he had nothing. No flares. A fire would take too long to start and his flashlight wouldn't do much in the bright sun, so he started to climb. Fast and furiously, he clawed at the cliff wall behind him, grabbing roots, branches, and crags as he tried to climb even higher. His fingers split open, his palms bled. The soles of his shoes scraped as he climbed and climbed. On a normal day, he wouldn't have been able to climb this wall, but with the adrenaline, he made it to the top. Ignoring the pain, he once again jumped up and down and screamed. The helicopter was veering away, cutting straight across in front of him; he just needed someone to look to the side and he just knew they would see him. Though he knew the screaming was pointless, he shouted until he coughed. His arms never stopping their frantic waving.

Seeing the helicopter stay on a path away from him, he fell to his knees once again. This was it, it was over. He had killed his fiancée. Looking back down the ledge, he didn't even know if he would make it back down to the ledge he had just climbed from. Maybe he should just throw himself down, die with Molly? Sitting down, he swung his knees over the edge and thought of the pain he was going to endure as he fell, the pain that Molly had already suffered. He would get hurt falling, but would probably land on the ledge above and have to throw himself off again. It was what he had to do, though.

"I'm coming, Molly!" he screamed as loud as his shredded throat would allow him. Sliding off the ledge, his feet hit the jagged wall first, jarring his legs and sending him head over feet into another rock. He felt the skin on his scalp peel back as the rock edge sliced his head open. Three more tumbles and he hit with a lung-busting splat next to the picnic he had set up. Opening his eyes was hard; he had never felt pain like this before. His mind was so foggy he couldn't even tell if he had blacked out or not. Wanting the pain to end, he knew he had to crawl to the edge and roll off to get to Molly.

If something was already broken, he didn't care. With nothing but his forearms, he dragged himself to the ledge, looked over, and saw Molly down there. She didn't have her eyes open anymore.

"I love you, baby," he whispered into the air. A fluttering noise started in his ears. Scared he might black out, he used all his might to roll off the ledge, hoping he wouldn't land on Molly.

When he awoke the next time, he had no recollection of the fall and was thankful for that. When he opened his burning eyes, it took him a moment to realize they had blood in them. It was in his mouth as well; spitting it out, he lifted his head and looked around. Somehow, he was below Molly by a good thirty feet. He could see the blood still dripping from her leg. She still didn't seem to be moving.

"Molly!" he tried to scream, but could hardly whisper as he realized there was a horrible pain in his chest that made him feel like he couldn't get enough air. The fluttering noise was still in his ears, only this time louder. It wasn't until he felt the dirt kick up around him that he realized the helicopter had returned. Lifting his head painfully, he looked above him and saw that it was now hovering there above him. He had gotten their attention! They were looking around for him! He tried to raise his arms, but they wouldn't move; his voice wouldn't obey, either. There was nothing he could do but pray they saw him.

After a few passes, it flew away. Chase started to cry, not knowing if they were getting help or giving up. As he cried, he turned his head to let the tears fall—they were pooling in his eyes and he couldn't wipe them. It was then that he saw the ring, the ring the he had hoped to see on Molly's hand forever. And now, instead, it was sitting still on a pile of pebbles.

Eight months later, Molly had her mother bring her to the graveyard. She had been in intensive care for Chase's funeral and in rehab at the nursing home for the last seven months. It was the first time she'd had a chance to see his grave. With a lot of effort, her mother pushed her wheelchair over the grass and left her alone in front of the smooth, black headstone. She read the date of his death, the day she should have cherished the rest of her life as the day she had gotten engaged. After a good cry, she caught her breath, stared at the stone, placed a few pebbles on top of it, and spoke.

"I never got to answer you, Chase. It would have been...yes."

LADY BUG

He concentrated on the blade of grass between his sore fingers. It was so perfect and, until a few seconds ago, it had been alive, just like *he* was. He kept staring at the blade, in awe of how he couldn't remember ever looking at grass so closely before. Why hadn't he? Why hadn't he taken the time to look at the world around him?

With a deep breath he raised his hand, waited for a breeze, and let the blade go. It fluttered down, shot up a few feet, and sailed away slowly. He laughed to himself. It was just too beautiful. Lying back, he enjoyed the tickle of grass on his ears and neck; he stroked it with his fingers and closed his eyes. It felt wonderful, like when he was a child. Thinking back made him remember the times he used to lie in the backyard with his mother to look up at the clouds. They would see rabbits, cars, ducks, and even flowers in the puffy shapes. Opening his eyes now, he felt a bit disappointed that there was only one cloud. A tiny puff of no shape in particular. He sighed and tried to concentrate on the warmth from the sun on his face. It was brilliant.

Twenty-six years of nothing but work. Again, he started to laugh. Almost three decades at one company and he hadn't once sat down in the grass like he did now.

Pathetic. He'd let his whole life slip away from him. The years all seemed to blur together. Like they were all just some long workweek. His failed marriages, his estranged children, all because he was determined to make it to the top of a company. He realized now what a fool he was. What was the point? Everything was over now, and for what? A savings and a 401K that he'd never get to use? They were worth nothing to him now.

Rolling his head to the side, he could see the top of a tree. A vague flash of a memory came back to him. Was it during his first year at the company, maybe the second? On Arbor Day, the boss at the time had made everyone go outside to plant a "company tree." Look at it now—thick, majestic, full, tall, and perfect. An angry tear spilled out. He hadn't stopped once in all those years to notice how that tiny sapling had grown, the same way his kids had grown up so fast. They seemed bigger each monthly visit. He could only imagine what they would look like now. He hadn't seen them in over three years. Would he even recognize them? Would they come and visit him after this? Probably not. They didn't visit now, so why would they visit after what he had done?

Hearing a siren off in the distance, he knew he only had a few more minutes to enjoy this moment. A tickle on his arm startled him; he lifted it and saw a tiny ladybug crawling over his hairs as if they were speed bumps. They were lucky, weren't they? Sitting up, he lifted his arm to his face to get a closer look at the tiny orange and black dotted bug. It certainly wasn't as cute as the dozens of ladybug items his secretary kept on her desk, but it was still beautiful. And lucky, right? He went to pet it with his finger but hesitated, afraid to disturb it. The sirens were much closer; suddenly, the bug stopped moving and turned towards him, as if to ask what the noise was. "They're here for me, little lady." He whispered. With that, the ladybug flew away. He tried to keep his eyes on it as long as he could, but it disappeared from sight, leaving the bloody body next to him in full view.

The look on the lifeless face was almost peaceful. He stared at it and smiled. "We're free now, buddy. I'm sorry, but it's better to be free." He stood up, turning to the dozens of his co-workers that were cowering behind cars and the police who were pointing their guns at him. Grinning from ear to ear, he put his hands out to be cuffed, truly seeing the world around him for the first time in his life.

FALLING STAR

"I'm a star, God damn it! I shouldn't be treated this way!" The scream came from down the hall. Mark rolled over to his wife, who gave him the look of death. With a sigh, he got out of bed, put on blue pajama pants and a T-shirt before brushing the lint balls off his shaved head. He was always amazed at how many stuck to his head after a night of sleep. There was another scream, but he was in no rush to get to his father—it was the same routine every day. After going to the bathroom, splashing some water on his face, and taking his morning vitamins, he headed for the kitchen—where his wrinkled, overweight father was sitting, wearing a coffee-stained tank top.

"You are starting early today, Father," Mark said, eyeing the mess his dad had made trying to make coffee for himself. He was going to have to make a new batch and make breakfast all while his father yelled and moaned at him.

"Christ, boy! I have been waiting out here for forty minutes—forty minutes! In my day, the maids had a ten-course breakfast on my table before I was even awake. Now? Now I have to wait like some schmuck to get a damn coffee. Humph!"

Mark bit his tongue. Every morning it was the same crap. His father would scream at him about how *good* life was, back *then*. Most of the time he could ignore his father's screams and move on with his day; other days, it pierced through his skull like an ice pick.

"Waffles, eggs Benedict, sausage, toast, marmalade—made by hand, mind you. It was a spread that used to make all the celebrities jealous. You know, Dean Martin once tried to hire Kathy away from me. I think that was her name. Anyway, after one crazy night, Dean woke up in my bathroom and went downstairs to find the spread. He thought he'd died and gone to heaven. The son of a bitch tried to hire her on the spot— I think he even offered marriage."

Pouring the coffee, Mark interrupted his father, "Let me guess, Dad. You walked in, heard what was going on, kicked Dean out, made love to Kathy atop of a stack of hot pancakes, and gave her a raise of five dollars a week. She stayed for the next ten years, am I right? For some reason, I feel like I've heard this before." He watched as his father scrunched up his face and poured an obnoxious amount of sugar into the coffee Mark had just handed him.

"By the way, Kathy is dead, you are broke, and I'm feeding you generic cereal for breakfast. Get over it." With that, Mark tossed a box of corn flakes, a bowl, spoon, and a half-gallon of milk on the table.

"It's serve yourself, too." Mark walked out with two cups of coffee and headed to the bedroom, ignoring the grumbling behind him.

In the bedroom Mark tried to ignore his wife's

menacing look. Handing her the cup of coffee, he tried comment about how nice it looked outside, but he was cut off.

"Why can't we put him in a home again?"

Mark sighed. "Because they cost a ridiculous amount of money that we cannot afford." He watched as Kathy put the coffee on the nightstand without taking a sip. Closing his eyes, he tried to calm himself. His father threw the same fits every day; then Kathy would follow with her fits.

"You know, it would be nice to go to a movie today or to dinner or to the park. Oh, wait—we can't, because we have to stay home in case your father tries to start another fire!" Kathy shouted as she slid down in the bed and pulled the blankets over her head. Mark blew on his coffee and took a few gulps. It tasted good. He thought of breakfast and what he might want to eat.

"You want pancakes today or egg sandwiches?" Mark asked to the lump under the blanket.

"Why do you always avoid this conversation?"

After another sip, Mark answered, "Because, it goes nowhere, there is no answer, and there is no reason to rehash it over and over again. Now, pancakes or egg sandwich?" There was no answer.

"Okay, we'll have pancakes." Finishing his coffee, Mark got up and headed to the kitchen. When he saw the mess his father had left, he forced a smile. So what if there was milk on the table, floor, and chair—and a trail of cereal flakes heading to the living room? Messes could be cleaned up, no problem; they just took time and patience. As he started to clean the mess, he heard a loud shatter coming from his father's room. In the back of his mind he felt pressure—a lot of pressure—trying to snap his calm, but he forced it down, took a deep breath, and walked calmly towards the noise.

"Damn it! Marilyn gave that to me!" his father yelled as he rounded the corner to the room. On the floor, he saw shards of glass—by the greenish tint, Mark recognized it as the perfume bottle his dad always had on his bureau. Mark remembered sneaking into his dad's room and smelling the perfume when he was a kid. The pungent smell hit his nose, bringing back memories.

"Monroe, Marilyn Monroe, Mark! Personally gave it to me after one hot night. I told her I loved how she smelled, so she gave that to me. Christ, the smell still gives me a hard-on and now it's gone. Gone because this shit-hole of a room is so small, I bumped into the dresser."

Mark felt a tremor in his hands; he was close, really close, to the snapping point. He didn't respond as he watched his father almost fall getting to his knees to sift through the glass shards.

"Dad, be careful. You can't cut yourself, you're on blood thinners. I'll get the dustpan." Mark felt something hit his back as he headed for the door. Turning around, he saw a small green shard hit the floor by his feet.

"I'm surprised you have a dustpan—way this place looks, I figured you didn't have one. Hell, I could leave this mess and no one would ever know it. You know, in my day I had a full staff of five maids and, by God, they cleaned every inch of my house—"

"ENOUGH!" Mark screamed so loudly that he blinked three times from the rush of blood to his face. Losing his breath, he felt the continuation of the sentence in his throat—it wanted out, but he swallowed it back. Rushing down the hall, he got the dustpan, turned back toward the room, and then dropped the pan on the floor. He needed air.

On the deck, Mark rubbed his hands together furiously as he hyperventilated. He had to close his eyes and count slowly to regain control of his breath. His father was going to be the death of him—hell, he was already ruining his marriage. By the time his breathing was back to normal his nose felt cold. It was going to be a nice day, but it was still early and cool. Hearing the screen door open behind him, he prayed it was Kathy and not his father. He couldn't take him again.

"Son…"

Shit. Mark could feel his breath start to slip away again. He thought about running to the garage, getting his car, and driving around for the day, but that would leave Kathy home alone with the menace.

"Yes." He refused to turn around and look at the man who was ruining his world.

"You know, son, Sammy Davis and I once got in an argument. Long story short, Frank was the judge and, well, I had a good inch-and-a-half on him. Now you may not have gotten my talent, son, but you inherited that. That is something to be proud of, you know? Size matters. Doesn't matter if you are a failure in life, you have that to be proud of."

Mark found his hand going to his own crotch. He moved it away and made a fist. What the hell sort of apology or pep talk was that? What was wrong with him? Turning around to ask him, he saw the screen door swing

63

shut.

With his blood settled down, Mark went into the kitchen and made breakfast for his wife and himself. He didn't offer any to his father. They ate in near silence. Mark lost the fake cheerful expression that he normally kept on his face. He was miserable and it showed, though Kathy did not acknowledge it. As Mark washed the dishes, Kathy cleaned the table.

Shutting off the tap, Mark took a deep breath and said fearfully, "We have to do something." As he stared at the water swirling down the drain, he felt hands wrap around his waist.

"I know. He is going to kill us if we don't." Mark grasped the hands on his stomach and held them tight. He wanted to turn around and look at her, but didn't know if he could handle looking in her eyes. Besides, the arms around him felt good, so he kept talking.

"There has to be some sort of home that won't cost us much?"

The arms squeezed him a bit tighter. "Mark, we barely get by as it is—anything would drown us. What happens to people who don't have families? There have to be places for them to go?"

Mark swallowed hard at the thought of his father sitting in his own filth in some disgusting place. "He was always good to me, Kath. How would I live with myself if I just dumped him somewhere?" He felt the arms slip off of him. The loss of pressure on his stomach made him feel empty as he turned around to see Kathy taking a seat at the table. She wanted to talk face-to-face, but he did not. Taking his time, he shuffled over and took a seat.

Avoiding eye contact, he strummed his fingers and waited for Kathy to talk.

"Damn dump! Toilet is clogged up, shit's flooding everywhere."

Mark closed his eyes, wanting to ignore the yell that came from down the hall. Opening his eyes, he saw his father shuffle out in boxers and wet brown slippers. The toilet *was* flooding.

"Let me guess, you don't have a plumber on duty. My old maintenance man could fix anything. Ever tell you about the time when Brando took a dump the size of Japan in my guest bath? Maintenance guy had to take apart the pipes to unclog that thing and that was before Brando got fat!" Fearful of ruining the hall carpet again, Mark jumped up ran down the hall and shut the water off under the toilet. It was too late, though—the bathroom was flooded and flecks of brown feces were everywhere. It was going to take forever to clean it up.

Two hours, one shower, and a new bathroom rug later, Mark was even more dead-set on getting his father out of the house. Cleaning up the man's crap from every inch of the bathroom had reassured him that it was the right thing, if not the only thing, they could do. The only question: Who would take him for free? Done with the cleaning, he decided to do a Web search for nursing homes in the area. Mark and Kathy had once used the third bedroom in the house as a computer room—that is, until Dad had moved in. Then it was used to store his father's stuff. The junk filled every inch of the room except for a small walking path to the desk and the desktop itself. Sitting down, he fired up the computer and rubbed his eyes. He didn't want to do this, but maybe it would solve things.

As the old computer took its time booting up, Mark looked around the room. It would be nice to have all the junk gone; he'd love to clean it up, make it *his* office again. A nursing home wouldn't let his father bring most of this. He could probably get his father to sell a lot of it, though—maybe make some money to cover costs. Curious about how much money he could make, he started to go through some of the cardboard boxes. Because he respected his father's privacy, he had never gone through the boxes. After two, he realized most of it was junk. Then, as he was about to set an orange box on top of a stack, he knocked over an old, wooden case that looked like a treasure chest. He had never really noticed it because it was behind another box. As it clattered to the floor, the tiny gold lock on the front popped off. Mark quickly picked it up. As he was about to put it back in the pile, curiosity overtook him. Sitting down at the desk, he set it in front of him.

He looked over his shoulder at the door. If his dad came, he should be able to hear him—he had time to take a look. Opening the lid, he first saw an old pair of panties. He quickly closed the lid, feeling like a child sneaking through his parents' drawers. Closing the lid had sent a puff of perfumed air towards his nostrils. It was the same scent he had smelled earlier, from Marilyn Monroe's bottle of perfume. He had to take another look. He opened it slowly and ducked down to look in, as if something alive might jump out. When the lid was fully open, all he could see was the pair of panties, but there was definitely stuff under them. Terrified that they were his mom's, he took a pencil and pushed them aside. What he saw made him gag, then scream with joy.

Pictures, a whole stack of them. At first, his father's naked ass smiling back at him triggered his gag reflex, but when he saw Marylyn Monroe half-naked next to him, ready to slap the ass, he knew he was going to be rich. He rifled through the pictures and had to keep himself from screaming with joy. There were over fifty pictures altogether, most of which featured Marilyn in various stages of undress. In some, she was doing very, very interesting things to his father. Half a dozen other pictures contained other celebrities, half-dressed as well and clearly wasted. His father's stories were true. He couldn't believe it.

Growing up, all he heard about was how wonderful a life his father used to have. How he was one of the biggest producers in Hollywood until he got blackballed for sleeping with the head of Warner Brothers' wife. After that, he couldn't get a job as a production assistant. Supposedly, he had financed a movie on his own that was supposed to be great, but the honcho at Warner Brothers stopped it from being sold. That is how his father had gone broke and became a car salesman, met Mark's mother, and settled down. The salesman dad, the only father he ever knew. The stories just always seemed like tall tales. Even Mark's mother laughed them off when he told them.

Mark trembled with excitement over the next hour as he rummaged through the boxes, finding item after item that would be worth a ton at auction. With tears of joy in his eyes, Mark set aside Marilyn's panties and did a search online. Sure enough, the story he remembered hearing was true. *Marilyn Monroe sex film sells for 1.5 million!* For a second, he lost consciousness; he couldn't handle the thought of how much all of the items in the room would go for. With a picture of Marilyn squeezing his father's nipple in hand, he raced out of the room and down the hall to Kathy.

His wife was lying in bed, reading a book and looking bored, when he burst in and started to dance in front of her.

"What the hell got into you?"

Mark held the picture up in the air. Kathy squinted to see it, then put out her hand to take it. After a few seconds of examining it, her eyes widened.

"Is that really her?"

Mark nodded and jumped up and down. "Problem solved! A sex film of Monroe's went for one-point-five million a year ago. In that room, there over fifty pictures of her and other celebrities—there is even a pair of her panties!"

Kathy got out of bed staring at the picture, she stood next to Mark breathing hard. "Wait. So your father—all of those stories are true."

Mark nodded and laughed.

"Shit, that is one hell of an apology we owe him."

As Mark and Kathy skipped down the hallway to apologize, they ran into Mark's dad standing in the office doorway, a stack of pictures in hand and angry tears welling in his eyes.

"How dare you! You went into my personal stuff! This is absolutely ridiculous!"

Mark stopped Kathy from talking and took the lead. "Dad, I'm sorry. It was an accident. I knocked over a box and they fell out. But it's great news! We can sell those pictures, Dad—for thousands. We can take better care of you now."

His dad grabbed the picture out of Kathy's hand, looked at it, closed his eyes, and turned back to the room. "Accident! Accident! I'll show you an accident, you ungrateful bastard." Before Mark realized what his father was doing, a cardboard box was on fire. "How do you like that for an accident!"

Mark rushed past his father, pushing the boxes over in hopes of dousing them, but instead spread the fire. The boxes, papers, and pictures were so old and dried out that they caught fire instantly. It was only a matter of seconds before the room was fully ablaze.

As the firemen shut off their hoses, Mark and Kathy held each other in silence. Their house was now just a pile of burnt rubble. Mark's dad was sitting on a neighbor's picnic table in the distance. Kathy and Mark shot him angry looks every chance they got, until finally the old man approached them. Mark whispered in Kathy's ear to let him handle it and got off the curb, letting the blanket fall off his shoulders. He stood tall as his father approached.

"I'm sorry, son. The house was a shit box, but it was still your home."

It took everything in his power to not punch his father. And, truthfully, the only reason he didn't was because he was afraid he'd kill him and have to go to jail on top of losing his house.

"You are on your own Dad, I never want to see you again," Mark said with his hand clenched tight.

His father nodded, pursed his lips, and looked away. "Okay, but you were so keen on these, you might as well have them."

Mark didn't care what he was talking about until he saw his father dig in his pocket and pull out the thick stack of Marilyn pictures. "You saved them?"

His father handed them over and laughed. "What? You think I'm nuts? Marilyn Monroe, naked? I'd rather lose my hand than those pictures. You know how many times I made love to your mother with one of those propped up behind the alarm clock to get me off? Don't think you are getting the panties, though—those are mine, damn it!"

Mark watched his father put a hand protectively over his pocket. *He saved the panties, too.* Mark laughed to himself. They might have lost everything in the fire, but with the insurance money and the money they would make on the pictures, they'd be just fine. But, most importantly, his father would be out of his hair.

JUST KILLING TIME

Mrs. Dale

I know this may seem like an odd letter, but please bear with me. I'm an old man and may ramble a bit, but I need to explain my reasons, so you know everything.

It's amazing how long a day can seem when you have nothing to do. When you can't sit long enough to watch television for more than an hour and can't sleep past six in the morning. When you have no one in your life. When you have no job. No hobbies and no family. My wife died nine years ago. We never had children (I wasn't able to because of a war injury) and my siblings have been gone for over twenty years. I'm eighty-seven, live on my own (just three buildings over from you), and I'm just killing time until I die.

After Kay died, I moved into this apartment building. The house was too much to care for. And, besides, why does one man need so many rooms? I hardly use the ones I have now. The sale of the house, along with our savings, gave me enough money to live comfortably—too much so, I guess. I'm too old to use it to travel, and I don't need anything, so I don't buy much.

71

At times it worries me, the money I have, because I have no one to leave it to. It's not a huge amount nowadays, but it's more than Kay and I made in five years (with both of us working when we first got married). That is why I have decided to do this.

Though it's not necessary, I have a routine. I wake up by six, lie in bed (achy and miserable for thirty minutes or so), get up, get ready for the day, and eat breakfast. After that, I go for a walk around the complex, more to stretch out than to stay in shape. By this time, it's almost seven. The rest of my day is spent reading, watching TV, eating, and going for more walks. I don't leave much anymore—I still have my license, but it's too stressful for me to drive. Therefore, I only leave when necessary, once a week for food and medications. It's a boring life; in fact, it's almost unbearable.

I have no one to talk to, no one to eat with, no one to call. I'm completely alone. The few friends I had are dead or in too bad of shape to go out or even use a phone. At times, I wonder if I'm being punished for something. For as carefree as my life is, it is hell. I pray almost daily for death, but it never comes. I have even stopped taking certain medications for weeks at a time in hopes of dying, but I guess I'm cursed with a strong heart. I contemplate suicide daily, but I never do it, for I want to be with my wife when I pass. The thought of being in purgatory without her is unbearable. I know this is morbid, but I need you to know why I would do this.

That is how it is. I'm stuck, bored, lonely, and miserable, waiting for death. I always try to figure out how much longer I have—five hours, days, weeks, months, or (god forbid) years? I thought once or twice about giving all my money to a charity, but not knowing how long I'll live makes that hard. And, besides, I don't trust them. You give your money in a matter of good faith and these non-profit places use it to pay the CEO a seven-figure salary. I couldn't stomach the thought of our hard-earned money paying for some rich bastard's vacation home. That's why I'm doing this.

The worst part about my situation is that I have way too much time to think. I've come to learn that my mind is my worst enemy. For I have nothing but time to think. Time has made me think of my life. All the things I could have done, should have done. All the things I would have changed. It's hard when you can't change your past and your future is almost over. It's these thoughts that made me realize, what have I done? I lived a good life, but I didn't *do* anything. I didn't change the world, I didn't shape lives. I worked as a mailman for over fifty years. It earned me a paycheck, but nothing more. It's not having a child—that is the hardest part, I guess. We always wanted them, we just never got around to adopting. We kept saying *next year*, until it was too late. I never realized that not having a child would mean I would end up alone one day, without a legacy to leave in the world. For when I die, no one will be at my funeral and no one will ever remember me. I will vanish from history. That is a hard truth to swallow.

That is why for the past eight months I have been trying to come up with something, something that will let me leave a mark on this world. Even if it's a tiny mark, I know now that I have to leave something behind—for if I don't, it would be the same as never existing.

I sit on my porch a lot and read; when it's nice out, of course. I have a ground-level apartment and my porch looks out into the small courtyard in the center of our buildings. It's nice, nothing great, but some green to look at. I was sitting there, staring out at nothing when I first saw Keisha.

The first time I saw her, I didn't think much of it. As she rode by on her little pink bike, I just thought, *What a cute girl.* That same day, she passed by my porch at least a dozen times. Each time, she waved to me and I smiled. I assumed she had just moved in because I hadn't seen her before. I went about my reading on my porch that day, but I paused to watch her every time.

It was summer and I assumed she was out of school, for she would play all day. She loved that bike. Circle after circle. And she was so polite—no matter how many times she went by, she'd wave or say hi. One particular day, she stopped and played on the green. I watched her as she chased after what I assumed were bugs for some time. When she got back on her bike, she noticed me standing on my porch and said hello once again. This time, I called to her and asked her name. She rode over and told me. I told her mine and she rode off.

The next day, each time she rode by, she said, "Hello, Mr. Murry." It was the beginning of our friendship. Little by little, as the days passed, she would slow her bike when she came to my porch and ask me questions. "What are you reading? What are you listening to? How old are you?" She was so inquisitive, a valuable trait in life.

Now I have bad eyesight, but the more time she spent sitting in front of me on her bike, the more I noticed bruises. Now, I may have not been a parent, and I know kids get bruises, but the number and location of these made me suspicious. I asked her one day about a large bruise on her upper arm. Her face went slack and a bit of color went out of her beautiful brown skin. She started to answer, but rode off instead. I felt bad for being intrusive, but knew something was wrong. It broke my heart to see such a beautiful young girl being abused. I didn't know the extent of the abuse, but I was determined to find out.

It took her three days before she came by again. And when she did, she acted as if nothing had happened. The bruise had faded, but this time I could see a fresh one on her thigh peeking out of her shorts. I didn't ask this time. Instead, I spent three weeks earning her trust. I gave her popsicles, played catch with her (the best I could from my chair—I can't stand for long periods of time), and chatted. During this time, I learned about you. She loves you, and you sound like a great mother. She didn't mention her father much—when I asked about him, I could see how uncomfortable she got and stepped around the question softly. I knew then that you were not the one hurting her.

A few more weeks went by and several more bruises came and went. Then, after not being around for several days, she rode by and waved very quietly. On her third time around, I got her to stop. My heart burst—her black eye horrified me. I asked her about it and she shrugged, mumbling that a ball had bounced back into her face. It took me a while, but I got her to finally admit the truth. I had earned her trust.

I don't need to go into the details about how her father hurts her; obviously, you know them. I may not know you or your feelings for him, but I know Keisha's. She is scared of him, hates him, and fears the few times he comes over every month. She is a wonderful girl. She wants to be a veterinarian when she gets older, did you know that? It's why she spends so much time outside collecting bugs and inspecting cats that are wandering around. It's a respectable job and she has a good heart for it.

Keisha needs to be away from this abuse. She needs to live a good life and have an education to make it in this world. She can accomplish her dreams and become somebody. I don't know your financial situation, but she tells me you work constantly and have little money for new clothing or much else. That is why I have decided to do the one good deed in my life for her.

I have written a check for Keisha. It's enough to pay for her college—even if she goes to an Ivy League, it is enough for room and board and so she doesn't have to

work. It is also enough for the two of you to put a down payment on a house of your own and to help you out for a long time. I will only give this check to you after you promise me two things. One, that you leave Keisha's father behind, cutting off all contact with him so he can never hurt her again. Two, you must promise to set aside half of the money I give you for Keisha's education. The other
half you can use for yourself and a house.

If you can agree to those two things, then please come talk to me tomorrow. I'll give you the check then. And don't worry, I don't expect anything from you and you don't even have to stay in touch with me afterwards. Knowing I did this is all I need in my life. For if you do those two things, I'll know I have affected a life in a positive way and that my life has been for a reason.

Please see me tomorrow. The check is already written and ready to go.

Bless you and Keisha.

James Murry
    Jamal squinted to see the name under the bloody thumbprint. James. He was a bit dizzy and confused at what was going on. He could hear Keisha screaming behind him. There were also other people coming—he could hear the bustle of panic, people rushing to help. He thought of running, but he also thought of the check. He wondered where it was. Should he search for it? Was there time? Damn it. Why couldn't he have controlled his

anger?

Anger had always been a problem of his, though usually he could stop just shy of doing something really stupid. This time, this time he had really blown it. Keisha had asked him to watch her ride her bike and meet her new friend. Of course, he didn't want to—why would he? Yet he did, anyway. He followed her outside, smoking a cigarette, and walking twenty yards behind her. When she stopped at that porch, he got suspicious. Who was this new friend? When he saw her climb over the railing, saw that old wrinkled hand scoop her behind to help her, he snapped. All he could think of was killing that sick old bastard for touching his daughter. It was a blur after that.

Leaping over the railing, throwing the man aside, kicking him in the ribs, watching the envelope fall to the ground, Keisha screaming. It was all a jumble. If had he stopped himself then, things would have been fine. But the thought of the man touching his daughter in worse areas flashed in his head. It was that image that made him do one fateful stomp on the man's head. He was protecting his child. He knew what he had done was right—until he picked up the letter addressed to his ex-wife. When he read it, his world came crashing down.

Someone was grabbing him from behind now. He could hear a siren in the distance, but all he could think about was the check he would never receive.

HOW DO YOU?

How do you tell someone? How do you express something when you can't even find the words? I have been waiting in the car now for seven minutes. Waiting. Thinking. Trying to figure out how to break the news. The news that hasn't even seeped into my mind yet, that I won't let break me down. If he sees me cry, it'll make it harder. I can't cry. I just can't. I won't. I won't.

Do I tell him soon as he gets in? Wait until we get home? Tomorrow? Should I have someone else tell him? Maybe the doctor? He should be able to do something like this with ease. Unlike me. I've never had to do anything like this, let alone deal with a situation like this. What about work? I'm going to have to take time off of work. I can't afford that. I have a huge project due next week. I'll never get it done. I'll lose my job, then I'll lose the house—everything will be gone.

Christ, will he even understand? I don't even understand why it happened. Why did this have to happen? Why me? Why now? I can't take this anymore.

I can feel the sweat starting to drip down my back. My hands are twitching and I'm blinking uncontrollably. All because I know he'll be here any second now. I should take him home first, then tell him. But then how would I

79

explain why I'm here and not her? I could lie? But what would that do but confuse him, maybe even make him angry with me? I couldn't handle that on top of all this.

An accident? How the hell do you explain an accident? One second our world was normal, and now it is smashed. All because of an "accident." Something stupid, so simply stupid it could have been avoided. I told her a hundred times not to drink coffee and drive. She'd spilled it—it burnt her and she swerved into the wrong lane while trying to wipe the scalding liquid off her lap. A simple accident. How do you explain that a cup of coffee took her away? A God damn cup of coffee.

I can see him now. This is it. He is almost here, smiling and skipping his way towards the car. I have to unlock the door. He tries the handle, but I didn't get it in time. With a click of the button, he lets himself in.

"Hey, Dad! Where's Mom?"

My tears are flooding out. I have to tell him. I tell him that my wife, his mother, is dead. I can see the confused look on his face. He's laughing as if I am joking. I let the tears fall and tell my six-year-old baby that it is going to be just the two of us from now on.

A FLOWER FOR MAE

It had to be perfect. It had to be the right color, the right size, and all the petals had to be there. Mae deserved the best. As Greg rode his bike, he could feel his heart thumping harder than normal for a bunch of reasons. One reason was because he was thinking about Mae, about how she would be so impressed if he got her the perfect flower. She certainly would pay more attention to him them.

The second reason for the butterflies in his tummy and heart beating fast was because he was about to ride his bike past the point he was allowed to go. Mother was very strict about him not leaving the street on his bike—*it wasn't safe*. He never disobeyed Mother, but he already looked all over the street for the right flower and just couldn't find one, not one perfect enough. He'd be careful, real careful leaving the street. He would hurry over to the park where he knew there were a million flowers, find the perfect one and get home before Grandma noticed he was gone. If she weren't babysitting him he wouldn't be able to sneak away like this. Mom kept an eye on him at all times—Grandma, though, she didn't want to miss her TV shows so she would only yell out the door for him every hour or so. That is why he waited to pedal fast as he could until right after he saw Grams go back in the house after checking on him.

Looking at his digital watch his uncle had given him a few months ago for his birthday, he figured he would need to be back in forty minutes at most. Should be plenty of time, the park was only four streets away. He was a fast rider. Fastest on the street, he should be able to get there and back in no time. With a deep breath he pedaled hard and fast past the point his wheels have never gone beyond. It was like being in a new world. He knew every inch of his street, every bush, rock, house and blade of grass by heart. What he was seeing now, though, it was all new. He had driven the street tons of times with Mom in the car, but never on his bike. There were no sidewalks, so even when he went bike riding with Mom they never went this way. It was so exciting.

Exciting that is until the first car raced by him. He was staying as close to the curb as he could, but even so, when the car went by and the wind slammed into his back he thought he got hit. He let out a gasp, stopped peddling, and started to shake. Maybe it wasn't a good idea, maybe Mom was right, it was too dangerous. Just as he was about to get off his bike so he could turn it around, he thought of Mae. It was her birthday tomorrow—if he didn't get her the flower, the one she showed him a picture of in class that she said was her favorite, then she wouldn't like him anymore. He just knew it. Billy was her favorite. He always bought her stuff, but Mom didn't have enough money to let Greg by things for Mae; that was why the flower was so important. Gripping the handlebars he started to pedal again.

Car after car flew by him, yet no matter how many went by he still jumped at the force of the wind. He was holding back tears now, but nothing was going to stop him, nothing. Not even the gigantic intersection he arrived at. Looking around in a panic he searched for a crosswalk; he knew how to use one of those. Mom always let him push the button, but this street didn't have one. On the corner he got off his bike, stepped onto the grass, and looked around. The park was still two streets away, but how was he going to cross them without a crosswalk? Patiently and scared he waited for the light to turn red. As he took a step forward to walk with his bike across the street, like Mom always made him do, a car flew right in front of him blaring a horn. He screamed and fell back on the grass, wanting nothing more than to be back on his street, the street he knew so well. Grasping at his feet, he made sure they weren't run over. Thankfully they were still there.

Trying to catch his breath he laid back and looked at the sky. There were a lot of fluffy clouds; they made him smile. Mae had once laid next to him on the grass and pointed out what the clouds looked like. She was so much fun. Sitting up he looked around again—there were still a lot of cars, how could he cross? It was then that he heard a voice from behind him.

"Hey...kid...you alright?" The voice scared him. It was a stranger, someone he shouldn't talk to—he would have to run from him, but run where? Turning to see the stranger, to make sure he was at least five feet away like they taught in school, he saw that it was a jogger. Some old guy all sweaty with headphones on. He didn't have a car so he couldn't kidnap him, right?

"Where's your parents? You shouldn't be on a road like this," the man said, out of breath.

"I'm going to the park." He watched the man wipe sweat from his face before responding.

"Does your mom know that?" Greg didn't want to answer the man; he took a big gulp, knowing he shouldn't lie.

"Yes, sir, she is there now. I...my friend's mom was supposed to bring me, but she was late so I decided to go myself." His heart thudded more. He never lied, he was no good at it.

"Tell you what, how about you ride next to me while I jog, until you get to the park. These streets are hard to cross, I don't want anything to happen to you." He thought about what the man said. He was a stranger, but he seemed nice and if he helped him cross the streets, he'd make it to the park just fine.

"Okay." He watched the man throw the earphones over his shoulder.

"Alright, stay next to me the whole time though, ok? And you stay next to the curb...don't cross until I say to." He listened to the man, happy to have someone to help.

When they arrived at the park the jogger reluctantly left them (thanks to another lie about seeing his mom by the swing set, a lie that he promised himself to go to confession for). Walking down the dirt path with his bike, he was no longer scared. This was familiar territory as well, not as much as his street, but Mom took him here a lot. There were so many flowers he didn't know where to start first. There were almost none by the playground so he decided to go by the pond; there was something Mom called the *rose garden* there that was filled with millions of flowers. That was where he would find the best one.

It took a while but he found his way to the garden with great excitement. There were so many flowers; he just knew the perfect one was in there! The picture Mae had showed him was of a purple flower, which made it easier to find the ones he was looking for. There were all sorts of colors everywhere. Colors Mae taught him about in class, colors she showed him that could be mixed to make new colors. He wondered if he put two flowers together if they would turn into a different color? He was going to try it when he looked at his watch and saw that he had already been gone for thirty minutes, he had to hurry.

Knowing there wasn't much time, he raced to the patch of purple flowers. He looked at them closely, swatted away some bugs that buzzed in his ear, and thought real hard about the picture Mae showed him. Was it the same one? It looked like it, he thought. There were two other patches of purple flowers so he raced to those, one after the other, to see if he recognized any of them. For the next twenty minutes he went from patch of purple flowers to patch of purple flowers, back and forth, back and forth. He couldn't figure out which was the one she loved. Panic started to fill him—he only had a few minutes left and couldn't figure out which flower to pick. It was then that he decided to pick one of each flower. Mae always said *you don't have to be right, but you have to try.* If he brought her one of each of them, one was sure to be the correct.

It didn't take long to find the first perfect one; it was so beautiful he knew that Mae would love it. He was careful to pluck it from the base like Mom taught him to do with flowers. Several bugs kept buzzing in his ears, but he tried to ignore and shrug them off. The second flower took a lot longer—there were so many of them and so many perfect ones hit was hard to decide, but he finally chose one and was happy with it. With only one left to get he looked at his watch and yelled when he saw the time. He'd been gone for well over an hour and Grams was going to be nervous. Knowing he shouldn't waste time looking through the last bunch he ran to the patch, a bit too quickly. With the two flowers in his hand he tripped and fell on top of the bed of purple flowers. Thankfully, he didn't let go of the two in his hand. Rolling over onto his back to get up, he felt bad about killing the flowers and panicked that he wouldn't have one to get for Mae. Though that panic was quickly replaced by a new one as a dozen bees suddenly
started flying around his face.

The first sting hurt so bad that tears instantly wet his face. The second one made him scream out loud and the third made him get up and run, swatting at the dozens of other bees that were covering his body. As he screamed and ran he could see people in the distance. He headed for them, hoping one might know what to do, like his mother would. Though as he cried his throat started to feel funny and he couldn't see that good. He tripped and fell again. When he tried to get up his arms wouldn't work—it scared him so much he tried to gasp, but air wouldn't go in his throat. Terrified and wanting nothing more than to be with his mom, he kept a tight grip on the flowers.

When he awoke he felt funny and heard noises like video games around him. Before he could open his eyes fully he felt his mom's hands on his face. He saw that she was crying and that scared him. Mom never cried.

"Why...why are you crying, Mommy?" he asked, scared and confused.

"I'm just so happy to see you, baby, that's all." After hearing his mother say that he fell back asleep and awoke over and over again. He just couldn't stay awake. During his awake time he learned that the bees had hurt him, that he was what Mom called "allergic" to them and needed to stay far away from them in the future. He never liked bees and now each time he fell asleep in the hospital bed (which was so cool with the controls) he had nightmares about bees—big ones—that were always after him.

Later in the day when he was fully awake, he was thrilled to see the flowers he picked in a vase next to him; he had almost forgot all about them and Mom had yet to ask why he had them. Though she did tell him that he would not let them go, not even when they took him in the ambulance (which he wished he remembered because ambulances were so cool and he had never been in one). When he was finally awake fully, his mom said it was actually the next day, but he didn't believe her.

"Honey, you have visitor." His mother who had been out in the hall talking to doctors said. Grams had already been to see him, but she had left because she couldn't stop crying, so he couldn't figure out who it was. When he saw who it was he heard the beeps on the machine next to him speed up.

"Ms. Mae! What are you doing here?" He did his best to sit up and look attentive like she told him he should in class.

"It's okay, you don't have to get up." Her voice made him melt; he loved listening to her talk, especially during story time.

"I... Hi." Was all he could manage to squeak out.

"The class and I were worried about you so everyone made you cards!" She lifted up a bag to show him; there was so many in it he couldn't help but giggle. His mom asked Ms. Mae if she would stay a few minutes while she went to the cafeteria to get some food. Ms. Mae said yes, his mom kissed him on the head and disappeared. He was nervous being alone with Ms. Mae.

"So you are allergic to bees, huh? My brother is as well. It's no fun, but you'll be just fine." He didn't know how to answer and he could feel his cheeks getting hot.

"I heard you were in the park alone. Why did you go there, sweetie? Remember what we talked about in class when officer Mattina came and talked to us? It's dangerous to go out alone." He looked away, feeling ashamed.

"I know...it's just I, I wanted to get you flowers for your birthday. Your favorite ones, there wasn't any on my street and I knew the park would have some so I...well I just...." Saying it, he remembered the flowers were next to his bed and reached over, stretching with a bit of pain to grasp them.

"These are the ones I got for you. I was going to get one more because I couldn't remember which one was your favorite, just the color. Happy birthday." Ms. Mae took the flowers. He could see she was starting to cry and felt horrible.

"I'm sorry Ms. Mae, did I get the wrong ones?" Feeling as if he might cry himself, he watched her wipe tears from her eyes.

"No, peanut, you got the right one. It's this one and it's perfect." He smiled so wide it hurt; he loved it when she called him "peanut."

"You know, that is probably the sweetest thing anyone has ever done for me, but you should never do anything that is dangerous like that again."

"I know, but I, well I lo…" Ms. Mae cut him off by putting up her index finger, the move that in class meant to be silent.

"I'm your teacher, peanut, and I'm much older than you. What you did was very sweet. You know, when you get older you'll make someone very happy." He didn't really understand why she was saying it, why she didn't like him more, but then she got up, leaned over, and kissed him on the cheek. The beeping next to his bed went crazy. And for that one moment all the pain and trouble he got in was worth it.

V.A.M.P.

Dear Media Outlets,

This letter will put my life and the life of my kind at risk. Please take it seriously and please help us.

This letter is probably the first real thing ever written about my race. I'm letting the truth out for the first time, because it is one of my only chances of survival. According to your beliefs, I don't exist—I'm what you would call a vampire, but my kind is nothing like you think.

Since that bastard Bram Stoker made that book of lies about us, our world has changed. Before it, we lived in peace. With the advent of movies, our world really came crashing down. Everything those movies and books showed you is wrong. In this letter I hope to clear things up, dispel some myths, and tell you what is really going on. I need to do this so that maybe one day we can all live together and I can be with the one I love.

To start this confession you must know some of the history of our kind and I must dispel some myths that your culture has made up about us. For one thing, I don't sleep in a coffin or live in some belfry. I actually have a nice loft in a small city that will remain unnamed (for writing this is dangerous for me). I live a normal life—in fact, you may even know me. I'm a food rep for a major wholesale food company and, no, I'm not that pale and don't have fangs. I'm just like one of you, just a bit different.

About three hundred years ago in Europe (country and town are arguable) there was an outbreak of a disease. Most of the town folk died, like the black plague, but a few survived. The few that lived were immune, but it still infected them. Instead of dying, their body started to kill off its own blood (this was learned years later). Somehow, one of these infected people realized that drinking blood cured them (for short periods of time), like a medicine. As these few affected people moved on through life, they bred and created a small legion of infected "thirsters," as we were originally called. They lived normal lives, usually getting by drinking the blood of pigs or cows they slaughtered themselves, bought at the butcher's shop—or, in some cases, they made deals with local morticians. Word of our kind did not spread for a long time.

It wasn't until Bram Stoker met one of us and made up his own story based on our kind (along with a mix of Vlad the Impaler) that our kind got such a vicious name.

You see, the best way to explain our condition is to compare us to someone that has a disease. You don't fault someone that has to take a pill every day just because his

91

body doesn't work correctly, so why should you fault us? We have a blood deficiency. The blood we drink is our medicine. And for those of you confused, yes, we are born; less than two percent of us are "created" like in the movies. I know this is a very layman's version of our origin, but I don't have time right now to get into details.

We don't have fangs. We don't bite people and suck their blood. In fact, a lot of us drink our blood from coffee cups, warmed up with a bit of sugar (my favorite way). Though blood tastes good to us, it doesn't turn us into animals, we don't hunt for it and viciously rip people apart to get it. We merely need it to survive and drink it as you would drink your coffee, which I would argue some of *you* need to survive. We only need about one gallon of blood a week to survive. We can get by with less, but that seems to be the optimal amount.

For the sake of time I will quickly answer the questions I know you are curious about.

Light: Though we are sensitive to it, it won't kill us. We take pills that help us with the sensitivity and use lots of sunblock. Most of us can go out just as normal as you. Though we do avoid days at the beach. And, no, we do not sparkle in the sunlight like that God-awful *Twilight* series.

Garlic: That is just flipping stupid. Though one friend of mine is allergic to garlic, but it's just a cruel coincidence and nothing to do with him being a vampire.

Paleness: You'd think that we are all pale and have black

eyes—well, at least according to the makeup artists on films. In fact, we all vary—some of us are pale like redheads, but some are fair and others dark. We come in just as many shades as you do. Our eyes look no different than yours, as well—mine are blue in fact. In a lineup you'd never be able to pick one of us out.

Crosses: Again, stupid and hurtful. Thinking that the one who created us hates us so much that the cross would burn us is a very painful issue with a lot of us, especially in a few sects that are heavily religious. Oh, and same thing for holy water—a lot of us bless ourselves with it, and it doesn't burn.

Wooden stakes: Yes, they kill us, and they would kill you, too, morons.

Eternal Life: This is one is half true. We can still die of injuries, sickness, and everything that kills all of you. The only thing is old age won't kill us. This is still being studied. And unlike popular belief, we do age; though in a way it's the opposite of dog years. Once we hit our twenties we only age, physically, one year for about every six-ten years. Again, there are many scientific theories on this that are still being argued. The oldest of our kind on record is 163. I myself am 71, but look to be 30.

Super strength: Nope. I'm actually a weakling. Another damn creative writer's imagination. In fact, the other day I couldn't open a jar of sauce; it was so embarrassing having to ask a neighbor.

Turning others into vampires with bite: This, too, is untrue. We are actually only born. Through two parents of the same kind. Which is why there are not that many of us. We can turn someone into one of us, but it would be through a blood transfusion (and one other complicated, forbidden way), and even then they wouldn't be a full-blown case. And if you think about it, if every time we fed we turned someone into a vampire, no humans would exist after a hundred years. I mean, do the math. If each of us fed on at least one human a week, starting off with a hundred of my kind, two hundred years ago, how many vampires would exist? Figure it out if you want—bottom line, you would be the ones on the edge of extinction.

Fangs: Normal teeth, folks, even had braces when I was a teen. Never bit a single person. Guess it made sense for writers to make a way for us to get blood. I did have fangs one Halloween when I went as a vampire, you know, to be ironic.

Undead: No, we are not dead and we do not come back from the grave. When we die, we are dead for good. Our bodies function just like yours; we just need that extra nutrients.

Turning into bats: If you believe this one, just stop reading this because you are too stupid to go on. Think about it, how the hell could a hundred-and-eighty-pound man turn into something that is about one pound? Where would all that mass go? Man, I hate these misconceptions.

Look, your modern day movies and novels romanticize

the ideas of our kind. Hell, though we are technically vampires, by society's standards, we don't even call ourselves that. We choose to be called, get this, PEOPLE, who have BDS (Blood Deficiency Syndrome). Your books and movies have caused us to live a miserable life style, one that I am now rebelling against, something that might get me killed.

Ever since *Dracula* was published, people have feared my kind. People fear what they don't understand. We went into strict hiding and started communities of our own, living off slaughtered cattle. We became monsters, devils, evil, simply because we have a deficiency. Our hiding continued for decades. It wasn't until the 1950s that everything changed. At first we thought it was a Godsend; now, I realize it
was nothing but an evil manipulation.

In 1951, Dr. Yamstal met one of my kind and talked him into being studied under the guise of helping us out and curing us once and for all (of course, many of us before this became doctors for this very purpose, but most of those doctors are insignificant). The government soon got wind of these studies. At first they panicked, realizing we were real; then they understood (so they said) that our lives were spent in hiding and that we posed no threats to the country. That is when they formed VAMP (Vampire Assistance and Maintenance Program), a top-secret agency to monitor and control the existence of all vampires (unfortunately, they call us vampires even though we have petitioned to be labeled with BDS disease and have been turned down three times).

As evil as VAMP is, it does do us some good. For one, they provide us with fresh blood on a weekly basis and the sunlight pills I mentioned earlier. Do you donate blood? When they thank you for saving a life, they probably mean ours. Forty-six percent of all donated blood in America goes to us. It works sort of like a methadone clinic for heroin addicts. Once a week we check in with our case manager (like a parole officer) at the clinic, who in turn gives us a gallon of blood. If we are in good standing we get the good stuff; it's sort of a rewards program. Follow the rules and you get blood from a twenty-something. If not, you get blood from that blue-haired seventy-year-old that donates twice a week. And, trust me, how blood tastes is a matter of age (though blood type does affect it a bit—I'm not a big fan of A-positive). It's like wine in a way, only the opposite—the younger the better. And the blood types are like the name brands.

VAMP also gives us regular checkups, which I now realize are for their own personal research and not for our health. The downside to VAMP is that you must register wherever you go and carry your VIP card (Vampire Identification Pass). And recently I learned that we are also embedded with tracking devices without our knowledge. It's that fact that is making me nervous now. When I don't show up for my appointment today, they will give me a two-hour window, then go after me. My appointment is in three hours.

Along with the benefits of VAMP, there come rules. At first, it was hard for my kind to get used to them after hundreds of years, but slowly they talked most of us into it, tricking us and forcing others to follow them. Most didn't care as long as they had easy access to free blood. Some of the rules are that we can't miss our checkups without written approval. We must never discuss VAMP with outsiders (a huge one I'm breaking now—the few that have tried have disappeared). And the most important one, we cannot fornicate with BDS-infected people. That is the reason I am now running. For I fell in love with a regular human for the first time, and I'm willing to risk everything to be with her. Convincing her that my story is true, that vampires exist and that I'm one of them, talking her into running with me, is what lies ahead of me. I'm not sure I'll be able to hide from VAMP—they will send its special teams after me, they'll turn my own kind against me, and they won't stop until I'm brought in or dead. If I had the powers you all associated with vampires, then I wouldn't worry, but I don't. I'm just a regular person with one problem: for the first time in my life, I'll have to find blood on my own.

I have no clue how this will all play out, if I will get captured, if Clarissa will believe and run with me, or if I will die from a lack of blood in a few weeks. I'm scared—terrified, really. I just hope that if I do die or disappear, then this letter will help start an investigation into VAMP, that the truth will be out
and my kind will be free for once.

Wish me luck, my friends, as I wish you luck in exposing the truth.

P.S. Enclosed in this packet is list of our clinics and people who work for them. This should be enough to get your research going. Please believe.

A HAPPY STORY

"Marvin, would it kill you to write a happy story for once?" Marvin sighed and ignored his mother. It was always the same questions when he came and visited. Every Saturday he would visit, she would hug him and tell him he was getting fat, and they'd sit down in the living room. She would then fire off the same five questions: *How is your girlfriend? How is the new house? How is your father? How are your feet holding up?* Then it would turn to the question about his writing. He was used to the other questions. He could handle them, and would answer: *She's good. It's a lot of work, but great. Same old Dad.* And, *feet are fine, Mother*, even though he never understood her obsession with foot health. For some reason, she liked to pause before asking the last question. Marvin always thought of the pause as her engine warming up to yell at him full blast.

"I don't write happy stories, Mom. you know that." At this point she would always throw her hands up and rock a bit faster in the rocker she hardly left.

"Why can't you be like Nicholas Sparks? He writes nice stories, happy ones."

"People die in his stories too, Ma." She sarcastically laughed him off.

"Yeah, but they usually end up happy. Not one of your stories ever ends happy. I don't even know why I read them, I get depressed." Marvin crossed his arms and looked out the window trying to not fight with her.

"You know I'm so proud that you are a writer, but I never tell my friends what you write because they would be appalled! They probably wouldn't even talk to me anymore if they found out about the filth you write." He couldn't hold it in anymore; she hit the spot that always made him fight back.

"Come on, Mom! I write horror. It's what the readers want. I'm published; I make a living of it, for crying out loud. It's nothing to be ashamed of." He checked his watch; it had only been ten minutes since he arrived. If he left any sooner than an hour, she would be insulted.

"Well, for once, can't you just write a happy story…for me? You know my birthday is coming up soon," she said in a cooing voice he remembered from childhood. He took his time replying. He was a writer—he could write anything, right?

"Fine, fine! I will write you a happy story for your birthday, but I doubt my agent will be able to sell it."

"I'm so excited, I can't wait to show the girls. See, I knew it wouldn't kill you!"

The next day, at his writing desk in the basement of his house, Marvin looked at the posters around him. *Death To All* by Marx Donavon, *When We Die* by Marx Donavon, *She's Dead* by Marx Donavon. Smiling, his eyes lingered a bit on the name. It still made him sad having a pen name, but like his agent said, Marvin was just not a scary or serious name. Maybe he could use it if this happy story turned out to be any good? Using that as his motivation, Marvin cracked his knuckles, straightened his back, and set his fingers on the keyboard. *Happy, Happy, Happy,* he thought over and over again. Nothing came. *Puppies, Flowers, Hearts.* Still, nothing came. Not one single thought.

Sitting back, he took a deep breath. Story ideas were usually his strong point. He had countless concepts stored away in files on his computer, but not one of them would be happy. Why was it so hard for him to think of a happy story? Why? Was his life that miserable? He knew it wasn't. It was perfect. He had a house, a great girlfriend, and an actual paying career as an author. He was never abused as a child, never had any great loss except his grandparents, but that was natural. So why couldn't he ever write anything happy?

This thinking session lasted longer than he thought it ever would. The tiny bit of light that came in from the small basement window had faded. Sitting in the dark near the cold, crumbly walls, he realized that might be the problem. He wrote in the basement, purposely keeping it cold, dank, and dirty to keep his mind in a dark place as he wrote. Change the setting and he should be able to change the mood. Grabbing his laptop he raced upstairs and plopped himself down in the flower-patterned living room his girlfriend had recently redecorated. It was bright, pretty, and feminine. This should do the trick.

After getting comfortable Marvin was excited; he was ready to write. Hell, maybe instead of a sweet short story for his mother he would write an entire new novel, a romance. He would use his real name. He'd get a new fan base of women and double his income with a new avenue. Maybe his mother was onto something. Relaxing, he took one deep breath, placed his hands on the keys, and they typed... *The woman was beautiful.* They typed fast and furiously, but when they hit that first period, they suddenly stopped. He established that there was a beautiful woman, but then what? Normally he would go on to talk about how her family died and they were coming back as zombies. He couldn't do that here. What would a beautiful woman do then?

His fingers left the keyboard to rest on his head. He stared at the flower patterns. Women loved flowers; they should inspire him. *Happy, Happy, Happy!* He repeated again and again. Nothing came. Frustrated, he typed again: *The woman was beautiful. The axe that smacked between her eyes ended that beauty. The End.* "Happy, Mother!" He yelled out to the room. Frustrated, he got up, paced and realized he was hungry. Time to make a snack. Maybe with some food in his stomach he could become a bit more sensitive.

With a bowl of black olives, a can of soda, and a bag of chips, Marvin sat back down and munched away. Usually, he never let himself snack while he wrote. It was a disciplinary thing; food was a reward for finishing. This was a new venture, though; his rules did not apply to this story. And it seemed to work, too—the food was making him a bit calmer. Maybe it was just hunger that was ruining his concentration. *Happy, Happy, Happy,* he thought with a mouthful of olives mashing together with chips. With a swig of soda, he picked the laptop back up. *Flowers, flowers, a florist...who falls in love with...a blind man who can only smell them. As she describes what each flower looks like to him, they fall in love.* It was perfect; this room, it did the trick. Laughing to himself, he couldn't believe he was ready to finally write a happy story. Mother was going to be so proud.

Marvin's fingers tap-danced across the keys, only stopping to pop the occasional chip or olive in his mouth. He kept smiling and laughing as he created a world for his unloved florist to live in. Being able to feel this good while writing never occurred to him. Usually he was in a dark, miserable mood to match his characters when he wrote. This was much more enjoyable. So much so he decided to go to Mother's when he finished to let her read it first, to thank her for opening his eyes. Laughing to himself he tossed an olive in his mouth and took a deep breath of joy, which was cut to short as the olive was sucked into the back of his throat.

Marvin coughed; the little bastard didn't come out. He tried to clear his throat; it was still stuck. Panic did not set in yet, but concern was rapidly falling on him. Calmly as he could he stood up then bent over to try and use gravity. Three loud hacks later he realized the olive was making no plans to leave his throat. Panic had arrived. With the lack of air starting to get to him he could feel his face get hot as he tried to think what you are supposed to do in this situation. Cross your arms and put your hands on your throat! Marvin did this only to realize that he wasted five seconds to do the international signal for choking to an empty room. A chair! That was the answer. Thrust your stomach on a hard edge and it will shoot right out.

Fumbling toward the recliner, he rammed his breadbox on the top corner only to have the chair move six inches. Three more attempts did nothing but rearrange the furniture. He had to get to the kitchen to use the counter. Turning, he saw bright spots dancing with black ones all around his eyes. The black ones looked ominously like olives. He took a step towards the kitchen, but it felt as if his leg sunk into the carpet. As he fell flat on his face, he hoped the impact would knock the evil olive from his throat. No such luck. Using the last of his air supply he sat up, his head drooping. His computer was right there in front of him on the coffee table, right next to the rest of the olives which now looked like spike balls. Marvin could barely see anymore, but he was able to find the right keys by touch to type his dying words. Slowly and painfully he typed;

Yes mother, it would kill me to write a happy story.

THE QUADRIPLEGIC
AND THE BOAT

Day One

As Carlos reached for the yellow rope that hung over the boat edge, his right foot slipped. It skidded out from under him, slamming him into the wall. For a second he laughed a nervous laugh, as he had almost fallen. When he lifted his left foot to regain his balance, that foot slipped as well. With his legs going in opposite directions he thrust his weight backwards in an effort to stop from pulling his groin, an action he would soon regret. When the middle of his back slammed into the low railing, he realized how close the edge was. As he tried to lean forward and grasp at nothing, he caught a view of the sky, then his feet sailing through it like two penny loafer seagulls. When his head hit the deck, his eyes winced in pain, but before he could even think about how much it hurt the weight of the rest of his body came barreling down on his neck. Hearing what sounded like a plastic cup being crushed, he lost consciousness.

When Carlos awoke, his head was throbbing. Opening his eyes, he had to squint, as the sun was beating down on him. It was then that he realized his skin was stinging. How long had he been out? Licking his lips that he applied balm to ten times a day, he felt that they were already dry and cracking. *Jesus.* He didn't feel any other pain, though. That was a good thing—just a head injury. Trying to get his bearings, he took a deep breath, but something didn't feel right. He took another breath. His chest, that was it—he couldn't feel it rise. *How odd.* Being right-handed, he instantly tried to lift that hand to his chest to see if he might have broken some ribs or something. Only his arm didn't move. It was such a simple thing, something he did hundreds of times a day and never thought about, yet for some reason his arm seemed not to be listening to him. Several more times he tried to lift it. Frustrated, he figured it must be broken. *Though, why was there no pain?* When he tried the other arm, he realized what might have been wrong.

Hyperventilating a bit, he tried to calm himself and move his toes…nothing. Legs…nothing. Stomach…nothing. He could lift his head just a bit, but fiery pain kept him from lifting it more than an inch to look at his body. Out of nowhere a scream escaped his lips. It wasn't a cry for help or out of pain; it was a scream of pure horror at the situation. The scream was so loud and long it set his head spinning with pain and tore his already rapidly drying throat apart. As he settled down, he felt tears running down his cheeks. They felt cool against the burn that was getting worse by the second.

As the tears dried Carlos took deep breaths, ignoring the fact that he couldn't feel them. *Maybe it was temporary, like some sort of shock, it'll wear off soon,* he told himself, though he didn't believe it for a second. He turned his head, ignoring the pain to look around him.

The fall had left him in the back of the boat, a small landing by the door that opened to the water to let swimmers in and out. To his left was the door that led inside of the yacht, where the bedroom and kitchen was. He was lying in an empty eight-foot by four-foot area. There was, though, a pile of yellow and blue rope a few feet from his head. Carlos stared at it, wondering how it could help him—but he knew that, only being able to move his head, there was no way he could drag his body two feet. Besides, even if by some miracle he did, what the hell would he do with it? Tie knots with his tongue?

Shutting his eyes to block out the relentless beating sun, he cursed himself. There was no way in the world he could be in a worse situation. The boat was afloat so far in the middle of nowhere that he knew no other boats would come near any time soon, if ever. He had chosen this spot for just that reason. Seclusion. As for the radio, GPS, cell phone, and transmitters, not that he could ever get to them, they were off. Again, a plan of his. So even if someone wanted to look for him, they wouldn't be able to get a signal. Not that anyone would be looking for him; he was off on vacation for a full week, and this was only day two of the trip. No one would expect him home for another five days and even then, no one would start to look for him 'til a few days after that. In this condition, he didn't know how long he would last. Not long, he hoped, for he had only been awake for a few minutes and so far every second was torture.

Trying not to think, Carlos drifted into a sleep as the boat sloshed, gently rocking him. It was a dreamless sleep, but when he awoke he thought he had dreamed his slip and fall. *It was a nightmare*, he thought as he opened his eyes and saw the stars glistening above him. It wasn't unusual for him to fall asleep on the deck. As he lifted his head, he saw his body twisted in a pile, his legs crumpled under the mess of his torso. *It wasn't a nightmare.* His head fell back; the pain filled it once again. As consciousness seeped back into his brain, he cursed himself for being so stupid. It seemed like such a brilliant plan; it would have been, if he hadn't slipped. Part of him felt like she planned this, that it was her way to get back at him. *Fuck you, Margaret!* he tried to scream into the night.

Day Two

Waking the next morning, the pain wasn't as bad in his head. Though his neck was so stiff he couldn't move it an inch in any direction. The worst part was his thirst. He would have sold his soul for a drink of water. As the sun started to rise higher, he cried to himself at the thought of baking under the rays for the next ten hours. Though he stopped believing in God at ten years old, he started to pray. He prayed with all his might...for death.

Death did not come that day, though at times he wondered if he was dead. He wondered if this was his permanent hell. Paralyzed, cooking under the sun's rays with no water or end in sight. Was that how he was going to spend eternity? Though he kept his eyes shut, he judged time by opening them every now and then to see the location of the sun. It was then that he realized how truly long a day was. With his skin drying by the second, starting to blister and crack, every minute felt like hours. He cried often, screamed in his head, and dreamt of being rescued.

Day Three

Sleep was nonexistent that second night as the boat rocked more and more, knocking his head side-to-side and sending waves of pain through his skull. As the sun rose, he tried to think of ways he could kill himself. He tried to swallow his own tongue, which was so dry and tacky that it did nothing but stick to his throat and annoy him more. As his cheeks started to ache from squinting hard to keep light out, he thought of a new plan for death. With all his strength he lifted his head and smashed it backwards on the deck. *Bang, Bang, Bang.* Over and over he slammed his head back until his energy ran out. The back of his skull got tender and squishy. It made him think of Margaret, but it did not kill him.

By late afternoon, the skin on his eyelids had dried to the point of cracking. Now every blink, every subtle shift of his eyes sent a sting across the lids. He started to laugh. He was going to die, finally, he knew it! He was going to dehydrate, any minute now, he just knew it. An hour later, dark clouds came in. The shade was like heaven; the rain that followed it was the greatest sensation he ever felt. With his mouth wide open he swallowed every drop he could while smiling and laughing. His face felt pliable for the first time in days and his throat wasn't a bed of razors anymore. As the rain came down heavier and heavier he drank more and more. The smile didn't leave his face; things seemed alright. *I'll get through this.* When the thunder clapped above him and the boat started to rock harder, his good mood changed to fear.

The rain was coming down so hard that it was impossible to keep his eyes open. Having had his fill of drinking, he shut his mouth along with his eyes and concentrated on breathing through his nose, which he had to clear water from with large huffs every few seconds. Suddenly, the boat started to dip hard to the side. He could feel his body slide a bit with the shifts—down, back, down, back. Carlos used to love storms at sea. Lying dry in the inside cabin, he would let his body roll and knock into Margaret; the two would giggle and giggle until they made love. Of course, that was years ago. This feeling, however, was eerie and horrible. Not being able to brace himself or shift his weight to stop the sliding made him feel totally out of control, which he was.

A giant wave came over the side of the boat, dousing him. Carlos gasped for air as he slammed into the back wall. The small, swinging gate popped open under his body weight. Lifting his head, he could see the water for the first time. White caps were rising and falling with anger. As he slid back the other way, his head hitting the pile of rope in the corner, he laughed to himself again. *This is it, this is how I die. I'm going to slide out and drown.* Part of him was thrilled that his nightmare would be over; the other part was terrified of drowning. The thought of falling into the water, not being able to move anything but his head as water filled his mouth and lungs…he couldn't fathom it. He didn't want to think of it; it made him think of her…*Margaret.*

Suddenly the boat sunk forward, then back. It was the deepest dip yet. As the boat smashed backwards, it rolled Carlos onto his stomach, but thankfully not out the door. He could tell his arms were crumpled under his body, as his head wasn't smashed against the ground. With his forehead lightly touching the deck, water sloshed across his face. He couldn't lift his head up high enough to pull it out of the water, so he held his breath. By the time the water flooded back out he was gasping for air and sobbing. The storm continued like this for what seemed like hours. He slid back and forth, held his breath, and gasped for air.

Day Four

As uncomfortable and painful as it was, Carlos was thankful for being on his stomach. At least now he didn't have to bake his face and squint all day long. Though after a few hours he did miss the view of the sky, and the pressure on his cheekbone was getting unbearable. Around noon, at least what he thought was noon, he started to hear noises. Scratching sounds coming from the deck above him. At first he ignored them, then he thought they were his imagination. When they didn't let up, he yelled at the noise, *Go away! Leave me alone.* He knew it was crazy, but part of him thought that maybe it was Margaret. That maybe all of this was her doing, that this was her revenge. *Margaret! I'm sorry, I'm so sorry…* His scream was cut off by the sound of flapping and a flutter in his peripheral vision. *It was birds!* He was too far out for birds to be around the boat, but if the storm had brought him closer to shore, he might be found.

You beautiful creatures, I love you! he shouted. Though he changed his mind the second he felt a sharp peck at the back of the head. *What the hell? Shoo! Shoo!* Another peck followed, then suddenly another bird landed, this one right in front of his face. Its mangy,

111

feathered head tilted and examined him before squawking a squawk that Carlos knew was calling others. He screamed, blew air, and spit at the bird in front of his face. It backed up a few times, but did not leave. It gained confidence and scooted closer. Carlos did his best to move his head at it, but it didn't flinch. Instead, it started to peck. At first, it was right next to his eye, a hair away from his temple. Two, three, four pecks. He screamed, spat, even tried to bite the grayish feathers that hit his face, but nothing worked. By the time he felt the blood trickling over his face, he could tell others were working on other parts of his body, though he couldn't feel them.

Each time one of them pecked his head, it felt like someone had jabbed sharp tweezers into him, pinched, twisted, and pulled it out. Over and over again. Out of the corner of his eye he could see one bird sitting on the railing, chewing on a chunk of his flesh, hair dangling from the piece. As two of the birds started to peck closer and closer to his eyes, he shut his lids tight and prayed they would spare him his vision. *Please, forgive me for my sins, but save my eyes, save them please*, he whispered as his lower lip was pulled out and split open. *Peck, Peck*. The filthy bird tore through his eyelid in two tries. It only took one to burst his eyeball open. As Carlos screamed and thrashed his head, the birds flapped their wings, but held their ground as they enjoyed their feast. He could feel several hot beaks enter the socket and gulp down the liquid of his eye. It took all he had to keep his other eye flush to the ground to protect it, but it was no use. It seemed to be the tastiest part for the fowl and they wanted more.

Day Five

The next day was spent in and out of consciousness. He had lost both his eyes, a lot of blood, half of his lips, and his nose and ears were torn into pieces. If he hadn't been on his stomach he would have choked on his own blood. During the few moments he spent awake each hour, his thoughts were hardly coherent. All he could see in his mind was the bird's and Margaret's faces looking at him. The two faces seemed to blend into one. They both had the same expression of horror, anger, and revenge.

The fifth time he awoke that day, he heard noises again. At first he figured it would be the birds. He prayed they would just finish him off, crack his skull open and eat his brains, but this noise was different. It was squishy, like wet shoes. *Margaret? Was it her? Was she not dead? She swam back to the boat, didn't she? She would help him!* His tongue, which had several splits and chunks missing, tried to form words without the help of his lips. They came out as slurs, but Carlos heard the words in his head. *I'm sorry I tried to kill you, Margaret. I do love you.* He swallowed and tried to move his head a bit for her to see him. *If it makes you feel better, it was your blood I slipped on, that caused me to fall and...well, end up like this. I wasn't going to throw you overboard, but I thought you were dead, with that head wound and all.* He tried to cry to show her he meant what he was saying, but without eyes it was useless.

"Jesus Christ!" The voice was deep and manly with a slight Boston accent. Nothing like Margaret's. It made Carlos's head swirl. *It wasn't her?* He lifted his head as if to see who it was.

"Jumping hell, he is alive! Boys, get the doctor and the board, we have a live one!" Carlos started to hyperventilate; he was being saved! He gurgled a yelp of happiness to the man who was his savior. Then, a thought came into his mind. *The evidence!* Carlos had fallen before he could clean up the evidence. The hammer that he had hit his wife with still had a chunk of her skull and hair stuck between the two prongs. There was blood everywhere. He was going to go to jail.

As he heard voices all around him he felt the sensation of being lifted, shifted, played with, and carried. He tried to speak, tried to beg them to not save him, to drop him into the ocean, but the words did not come out right. They merely hushed him. Then someone, who he assumed was the doctor, whispered in his ear.

"Don't worry, lad, it might seem bad now, but you are going to live a long, healthy life." Carlos let out a bloodcurdling scream as he realized that the rest of his life was going to be spent blind, disfigured, paralyzed...and in a jail cell.

The Lighter Side

THE MISADVENTURES OF A BABY-KILLING BOYFRIEND

"How the hell do you think I got pregnant, you moron?" As she screamed at me her curlers bounced around and spit shot from her mouth like one of them lawn sprinklers. I was offended by her wisecrack, so I tossed aside my bag of Cheetos, placed down my Diet Dr. Pepper, and stood up with authority. Being six-five, I always hit the ceiling on the trailer. The tingly feeling in my noggin distracted me for a second, but after the sensation was gone I remembered my comeback.

"I *know how* you got pregnant, I just don't *understand* how." Finishing my pointed remark, I crossed my arms and tried to raise an eyebrow to show her that I had made my point, but couldn't. I have never been able to do that. Wish I could though—people with raised eyebrows always look so cool. It was when I was trying to think about different cool actors who could raise their eyebrow when the phone hit me. Right in the eyebrow I was trying to arch. It hurt like hell and I cursed up a storm to tell her so.

119

Sitting back down to nurse my wound and eating another one of my cheesy friends, I watched Tina calm down a bit as she sat on the new stool I had stolen from a neighbor.

"Look Ricky...we are going to have us a baby. You're gonna be a daddy! We'll be a family!" Finishing a swig of the Doctor, I thought of a logical question.

"Now why the heck would we do that? That Planned Mom place or whatever it's called rips them suckers out for free! I'll even go with you if you want. Just not tomorrow, I'm planning on going fishing..." That was when something else hit me in the head—not sure what it was that time because I blacked out.

When I woke up I was pissed; my Cheetos were gone. And I had a headache, which reminded me of what was going on. I was in a real pickle. I was supposed to break up with Tina days ago, but truthfully I haven't had the balls to do it. Plus, she has cable in her trailer. (I hated missing my soaps—you miss one and you're confused for weeks.) Every night after Tina went to work, I would sneak over to Kiki's trailer. First thing she would do was ask me if I broke up with Tina yet. When I said no, she'd slap me, but then quickly hug me and apologize. Then she'd push me away again, yelling at me in Spanish that I can't understand, then she'd screw me good. It was sort of our routine. Though I knew it wouldn't last much longer because she was starting to talk about telling Tina herself that we were planning on getting hitched. Now with this whole mess, Kiki was sure to flip. I had to do something; I couldn't lose Kiki! She was my companion for life. I knew this before I knew her name, the first time we had sex in fact.

I got up carefully and went to the bedroom, which was only four feet away. Stepping through the beaded curtain, I could see Tina's hundred-pound, six-foot frame (our friends called us the Green Bean Gang) stretched out across the twin bed. Thankfully, she was on her stomach, so I didn't have to look her in her face. Eye contact sucks when you have to lie or talk about something serious like how you clogged the toilet. Sitting down on the bed next to her, I saw my empty Cheetos bag by her head. It pissed me off but I bit my tongue. Then, before I could even open my mouth, she spoke harshly to me.

"You ever mention getting rid of little Clever again and I'll kill you so fast you won't even be able to...to do something. I swear!"

"You already know it's a boy?" I asked, trying to change the subject—and it seemed to work. She propped herself up on her elbow. Her face was covered in that black makeup from her eyes.

"Well, no, but I just feel it. I know he'll be a boy." I looked down at her bare stomach; she was rubbing it. It was still flat and thin as a ruler, so I was a bit confused at how a baby fit in there. He had to be as skinny as Tina.

"How pregnant are you? You don't look it." She rolled her eyes at me.

"A week, maybe a day or two more. I think it was when you did me behind the trailer last Thursday. Remember, Mrs. Claire's cat kept trying to lick your coin

121

purse?" I did remember that time. We were doing it outside because Ma was visiting and we had no privacy.

"Well, are you sure, that you are sure, that you are pregnant?" Again she rolled her eyes.

"Yes! A woman knows and I took one of them EKG test stick things. I stole it from the drug store. Those tests don't lie!" Hearing that, I knew it was the real deal. So I tried to go a different angle with it.

"We can't afford a kid, those things are expensive as hell, darling."

"Not really. I'll have a baby shower and get all the crap we need for him, then the government will cut us a fat check every month to take care of everything else. Sally down the road gets, like, ten checks and food stamps for her kids. That's how it works, ya know. You won't have to pick up any more days at Dale's. I know how you don't like to work more than twice a week and, heck, with a kid you might be able to take even more time off." She had a point. And I was painting myself into a hallway.

After she went to work that night, I strolled over the two trailers to Kiki's and we went through our routine. As we lay on the kitchen floor catching our breaths, I thought it was a good time to bring up the subject. Pop always told me that if I had something bad to tell a woman, tell her after we bumped uglies. So that's what I did. After a string of Latina obscenities, she hit me in the head with her high heel (the one that fell off while she was doing the splits). I didn't pass out, but it did aggravate my headache.

"How could you do this to me?! How far along is the bitch?" I dreaded that question and tried to change the subject by telling her how hot she looked standing above me naked with one shoe on and the other in her hand. That brought another blow to the head.

"How far?!" Covering up my head and curling into the fetal position, I whispered how long. Amazingly, nothing hit me.

"Good!" I was confused at her reply. "That means we have time. You have to talk that slut into getting an abortion." Sitting up, I smiled at her and explained that I already tried and that there was no way. The shoe hit me again.

"What's the bitch afraid of? It's nothing. I've had like six or eight. Tell her they don't hurt. And sometimes they'll give you free drugs when you leave."

"It's not that...she wants to have the baby."

"Well, I ain't marrying a man with no baby. No, sir. I don't want no broken home. You are going to fix this! You are going to kill that thing."

"How can I do that?" She crossed her arms, leaning heavily to her left because, without that one shoe on, she was four inches shorter on that side.

"Uh...Well, you can give her some poison or something."

"Wouldn't that kill her too? I ain't going to no jail. You really want a hubby behind bars? They only give you, like, one of them bang visits a month. You wouldn't be able to handle that."

"They make pills and things that could kill the baby and not kill the slut, just make her sick. We could give her some of that stuff."

"But wait a second. Is killing a baby murder?" I asked her with all seriousness.

"No, you idiot! It's not real until it's born. So it don't count as nothing. Besides, it ain't human until it comes out. When it's in the belly it's considered an organ or some shit." She had a point and, with that, our planning started.

Two days after first hearing the news, Tina was already telling everyone we knew. Which didn't ease my pressure at all. The plan Kiki and I came up with was pretty simple. I was to mix some bleach into the orange soda that she drank while we watched our soaps every day. Kiki thought she had heard about someone who drank some once to get rid of a baby and that it worked. So we figured I should give it a whirl.

Tina was sitting on the couch with her feet up holding her belly with pride. She had already been telling me not to smoke around her (like that mattered, my momma smoked like a chimney when I was in her) and bossing me around saying, "I'm pregnant. I shouldn't be doing nuttin'."

So as she sat on her ass and I waited on her hand and foot, I cracked open an orange drink and poured out half of it. Then I ducked down behind the counter and poured some bleach into the can. (I had to go out and steal a bottle from the convenience store since we didn't have any.) A bit of it spilled on my fingers and stung, so I quickly wiped my hand and the can on my shirt and stood back up. Walking back towards Tina, I was sweating a bit and trying to act cool as I possibly could.

"Here, peaches, got you your soda."

"Thanks, pookie bear," she replied without looking as she grabbed the can. I sat down on the stool, waiting to see what would happen. I didn't know if something would start immediately of if she'd just poop the baby out later.

"Christ on a stick, Ricky! Is this bleach?" I was busted, but I couldn't admit it.

"What the hell are you talking about, honey?" She sniffed the can, then held it out in front of her with two fingers.

"What are you trying to do?"

"Huh?" I didn't know what to say. She stood up quickly and stared at me with a look that usually ended up with me unconscious moments later.

"Are you trying to poison me? Is that it, Ricky?"

"Honey, I have no clue what you're talking about. I just opened that can, it should be fine."

"Then why do you have a bleach stain on your shirt, dumbass?" I looked down at my favorite black T-shirt and, sure enough, there was a huge, peachy-colored smudge right by my left nipple. I still wasn't ready to admit it, though.

"Well, you do the laundry, honey, so you must have done that."

"You didn't have it five minutes ago and we don't even have bleach! You know I wash your shit in the sink with the dish soap," she screamed at me, getting even more annoyed. I was scared.

"I swear to you, baby love, I didn't do anything."

"Then drink it…prove to me nothing is wrong." Wanting to show my innocence, I grabbed the can and chugged it with four solid gulps and threw it down. I had proven my point!

"There! You happy now? See, nothing wrong!" Then, my throat suddenly felt like it was on fire, and I couldn't breathe really well.

"Baby? Oh God, baby!" Tina cried, grasping my face. The last thing I saw was her running out of the trailer, yelling for our neighbor who had a phone to call an ambulance.

When I woke up, Tina was standing above me. I was in the hospital.

"Baby! You're awake! God, I was so worried. Don't worry, though—we are going to sue them damn soda makers! We'll be rich." I tried to speak, but it felt like I had a bad sunburn in my throat.

"Don't try to talk, baby, don't." So I didn't. I couldn't believe how much damage the stupid bleach had done to me. I hadn't even thought I would taste it. The doctors came in and explained that I shouldn't talk for a few weeks, and that I could only eat soup and what-not for just as long.

After three weeks I could speak, but pretended I couldn't for another two to stay out of trouble with Tina, who was redoing a corner of the trailer, making a nursery while working on a case with one of them TV lawyers against the soda company. He told her we had a great case and should be millionaires any day now. I just nodded when he asked me questions and took pictures of me looking all sad. The sadder, the better, he said.

During that time, Kiki was even nice to me. It was actually a pretty good month. Though it had to come to end, of course. Once Kiki realized I could talk, she went right back to nagging me.

"The bitch is still pregnant. I think I can even tell now, she looks fat as hell. What are you going to do about it?" I held my throat and pretended to not be able to talk. She slapped me and said to stop that shit.

"Well, you're the one that wants the baby gone, so you come up with something." It wasn't the right answer.

"What? You want me? Don't ya, baby?" She purred as she touched my stubbly face. She was so beautiful.

"Of course I do, honey."

"Well, I won't go out with a man who has babies running around all over the place. So if you don't get rid of that kid, then you won't have me!" It was said in such a way that I knew if I did anything but agree, I was going to get a beating—so I agreed.

"Now, I remember seeing some movie once where a woman fell down the stairs and she lost her baby. Maybe you could…you know…maybe push her down the stairs or something. She'd only have a few bruises, but I bet it would pop that piece of crap out of her like nothing!" I thought about it for a few minutes. Sounded like a good idea. And should be easy enough to make it look like a mistake as well. There was only one problem.

"But, K, our trailer only has three steps. Think that'll be enough to do it?" She crossed her arms and gave me that look that always made me feel pretty stupid. I hated that look.

"I didn't mean your trailer. You need some good steep stairs. Like, uh, the mall or something. They have them big escalators. You could do it there. Just make sure it looks like an accident—there will be witnesses there." My baby sure was a genius. It was a perfect plan. Besides, what could go wrong?

Two days later, I talked to Tina. She was so excited and said how the baby missed hearing my voice. The thought of that creeped me out a bit. So I suggested to her that we should celebrate getting my voice back.

That we should go out to a fancy dinner. So we went to the mall to go to Ruby Tuesday's (one of you can get the salad bar and then you both eat from it to save money—hell of a deal, really). The meal was pretty darn good. It always amazes me how them fancy places can put together things you never thought would go together.

After eating, I suggested we walk around the mall a bit and look at things to get the baby. This made her happy. So store to store we went. It was so boring, looking at all the tiny things that cost a million bucks. Who would want to waste such money on a kid when you could spend it on yourself? Anyway, I finally got up the courage for the big push.

"Hey, let's go to the toy store downstairs. Maybe we can get something for the nursery." This got me a kiss on the cheek. As we reached the top of the escalator—you know, one of those super-long ones that take a good minute or two to go down with the glass sides. Like a gentleman, I offered for her to go first. Everything was all set. I took a quick look around to see if anyone was paying attention to us, and no one really was. My plan was to pretend to lean over to tie my shoe and fall onto her, at which point I would actually push her down the stairs but hold on to the railing myself.

The moment was upon me. I crouched down a bit, grabbed my shoe, pretended to wobble, and threw myself forward. Now, I should have made sure she was still in front of me, because she wasn't. Excited by the toy store, she ended up looking over the railing, trying to find out where it was. Which meant when I lunged myself forward there was nothing to stop me. I flew down five stairs and hit my face right on the edge of one of them metal steps. You ever notice how sharp those suckers are? Especially with the grate pattern they have. Well, it darn near skinned my face, not to mention it broke my nose in three places. From there, I don't remember much, but I'm told that I flipped over myself several times and that was how I broke my arm and shinbone. But that's not the worst of it. I guess when I landed at the bottom, the stairs kept moving, basically crushing me into a ball. Hence how I got seventy-eight stitches along my side. But the most embarrassing part was that it grabbed hold of my black jeans (which were three sizes too big, you know the style) and ripped them off of me, leaving me bare-ass since I had no underwear on—we were behind on the laundry. So, in other words, I lay there naked and bleeding while a crowd gathered around. I can only imagine how much they laughed. It even made the news that night—some punk kid had one of them phone cameras and got a good shot of me lying there. I never got to see it, though, because I can never figure out what time the news is on.

The next time I woke up, I was once again in the hospital. I woke up to flashbulbs popping in my face. The slimy lawyer that was doing our soda case was acting like some famous photographer, telling me to look as miserable as I could. That wasn't too hard. No one even asked me how I was as I awoke from my slumber. Tina and Sloan—I think that was his name—just kept telling me how we were going to own the mall when he was through with them. The thought of being rich was great, but I was in so much pain I didn't care and passed back out.

By the time I was back in shape to do anything, Tina's belly was getting pretty darn big, and she was packing on the pounds. She was almost to a disgusting hundred and twenty pounds. I was getting pretty grossed out, so when I came back home I started sleeping on the couch, giving the excuse that she needed the room in bed for the baby to grow. Probably the best thing about falling down the escalator was everyone treating me like a prince. I was waited on hand and foot for months! A man could get used to that sort of life. And one thing it did do, it reassured me that I still had to get rid of the baby. With a kid I'd have to do things like...feed it or play fetch with it or something. That wasn't my style. So it was back to the drawing boards.

Kiki had been thinking the whole time, and the best thing she could come up with was some sort of impact to the belly. She said poison now would just make the thing retarded. And that would just make things even worse. Besides, after the escalator incident I wasn't too keen on attempting much myself, so Kiki reluctantly agreed that this time she take a whack at it, literally.

The new plan was a bit blunter than the other ones. And it involved a certain degree of risk. Yet it was easier than the others. Basically, Kiki was going to get one of them ski mask things, put it on, and wait by our trailer door with a baseball bat. When Tina opened the door and walked out, she would swing it right into her big belly, grab her purse, and run off. The police would think it was a robbery, the baby would be gone, and we'd get a few extra bucks as well. It was brilliant and easy. I only wished we had thought of it earlier.

The first problem we ran into was the mask. Being still warm out, we couldn't find a ski mask anywhere. So I suggested using pantyhose like in those bank robbery movies. But Kiki only had fishnet stockings, which didn't really cover her face but did turn me on. (We had sex before she took it off, and it was hot!) My next idea was a plastic bag. We could cut eyeholes out of it and it would hide her face perfectly. So I tried it, since I was the one who came up with the idea. It worked pretty good—only thing was, the eyeholes kept moving. To fix this problem, I merely tied the handles together behind my head. Getting up to go look into the mirror and make sure it looked good, I started to sweat a lot and got a bit dizzy. I instantly blamed the five beers I had drunk before putting it on.

Well, I didn't make it to the bathroom. Once again, the familiar feeling of blacking out took me over and I collapsed in the kitchen. Luckily, the crunch under me woke me up enough so I could rip the bag off my face. I never realized how much I liked air. It wasn't until I had the bag off that I realized whatever I was lying on wasn't too comfortable. Rolling onto my side, I noticed my wife beater had splats of red and fur on it. It took me a few seconds to realize I had landed on Tito, Kiki's Chihuahua.

I must have landed on him just right, because I'm not a heavy guy. I never knew falling on something like that could crush it; I mean, he popped like a watermelon. I stood up fast as I could, grossed out from all the goo. Thankfully, Kiki was in the can. (We'd had Spam for dinner. It always gave her the squirts, but she kept eating it anyway because she loved it). Which meant I had a max of twenty minutes to clean up the mess and pretend I had no clue where Tito was. It wasn't easy. I had to use a spatula to get him up off the ground. Not thinking, I threw what was left of him in the bag that was still on the floor. I was racing for the door to throw him in the pond out back when chunks of Tito flew out of the ripped bag and splattered against the wall. I used my shirt to wipe it off.

Satisfied that the mess wasn't noticeable (and if there was some left, my excuse was going to be that it was spaghetti sauce from the can of SpaghettiOs we ate as a side dish to the Spam), I ran out the door, down the path, and threw the bag into the water. It didn't sink. But that didn't matter—there was so much trash floating in it that no one would notice the difference. The spatula sunk instantly, though. Next was my shirt. I tossed it in and that actually sank pretty quickly. Then, I cleaned myself up with the water and ran back to the trailer. Right as I shut the door, I heard the toilet flush. I dove onto the couch and pretended nothing was wrong.

Sitting down next to me on the couch, she sighed with relief as if it was a battle in there and she had won.

"What the hell is that smell? I know it ain't my

shit. Damn, boy! You crap yourself while I was in there?" Still breathing hard, I hadn't noticed that I stank from the pond water I had used to wash up.

"Oh...uh, I did some pushups. Must be b.o." She moved away from me and luckily didn't mention it again.

"Tits...here, Tits, Tits." It was what she called Tito. I gulped but ignored her calls.

"Where the hell could she be?" I shrugged.

"Maybe she found a piece of Spam on the floor or something," I suggested. She shrugged.

"So the plastic bag work?" I almost cried when she asked, but I held myself up high and grunted, "No."

"Maybe a paper one?" I nodded but let her try it out. She cut two eyeholes and plopped the bag on her head. With her rather large hairdo, it didn't move at all and she could see just fine.

"Looks like that will do. You'll only need to have it on for a few seconds, anyways." We agreed and I snuck off to take a shower.

Two days later, we were ready with our plan. I was to stay in the trailer with Tina before she left for work as an alibi. Sitting on the couch, I sucked back the Cheetos and tried to act calm while Tina was getting ready in the back. To save money, she wasn't buying any new clothes to accommodate her large stomach. So her bare belly stuck out of her outfit. It would make a good target for Kiki. Tina was running behind because of that clothing issue, and I wanted to make sure Kiki hadn't left thinking she missed her, so I opened the door and took a step down. Another brilliant mistake.

Since Kiki decided on the paper bag mask, she didn't have much vision. Well, not as much as she thought. That, mixed with the fact that she wasn't expecting me to come out of the trailer, was her excuse. Her excuse for swinging the bat, which unbeknownst to me she had altered a bit to make it more effective. She had pounded a half-dozen nails into the head of it to make sure that they would pierce through Tina's stomach and get rid of the baby once and for all. Well, let me tell you, they would have worked.

Kiki had summoned some superhuman strength. She shattered my pelvis bone, and the spikes pierced my innards in several places. And, of course, as I fell to the ground I once again fell on my face, breaking my nose. Kiki told me later that, after hitting me, she panicked and ran to the pond to toss the bat and mask before hiding out in her trailer for a week. Luckily for me, Tina found me on the ground a few minutes after it happened, and once again she ran to the neighbor's to call an ambulance.

By this point, we were racking up a hefty medical bill, well over six digits. *But don't worry! Oh no, no, don't worry at all,* the sleazeball lawyer told me as I woke up once again in the hospital. He went on to tell me we had a third lawsuit going, this time against the trailer park for having inadequate security. I was going to own that trailer park, along with the mall and the soda plant! Or so he told me as I drifted in and out of consciousness between the half-dozen surgeries it took to fix my intestines and replace my pelvis bone with a titanium one.

For some reason during this hospital stay, which was a long one, Tina visited me less and less. And, in the end, she was really only coming once a week. I was fine with that. Kiki was coming every other day and sobbing for the first hour with apologies. Then she would try to get me off, but I had a tube in my schlong for the first few weeks, so that ended in her being covered in piss and me in pain—at least the first four times we tried. Then, as our routine went, Kiki would start to curse out Tina. She figured she must have found out about the plan and taken her time so I'd fall into the trap. She also came up with the theory that she got herself pregnant because she knew I was going to leave her. Every night, Kiki got angrier and angrier. So much so that she even talked about killing Tina. At first, she was just kidding. But as the days went on, I knew she was serious about it.

I didn't like the idea of killing Tina. Mostly because I didn't want to go to jail. I wasn't going to be anyone's bitch—no one tells me what to do!

"Sit up straight when I'm talking to you. Now, listen, this is what we are going to do. I don't care what you think, this is the plan."

"Yes, my love." Kiki was serious, and what finally convinced me to go along with the plan was the fact that Kiki brought up: if Tina was alive, then she would get half of all the money I had coming to me from the lawsuits. I didn't want that to happen. So I agreed to the new plan. This one was the best yet...foolproof.

This time when I got out of the hospital, Tina was like a hot air balloon. She waddled when she walked and, thankfully, didn't want to have sex anymore. Though I was curious what it would have been like. My first day back in the trailer wasn't comfortable. My body was having a hard time digesting things, so I spent most of the first night in the can. At one point, Tina came in and screamed at me because she had to tinkle. As I stood outside of the door with my pants around my ankles out of fear of something oozing out of me, she apologized and said the hormones were killing her this last month. I had no clue that much time had passed. I was shocked to find out that she was due in a few weeks! Kiki and I were going to have to push up our plans.

That night, after Tina went to work, Kiki and I planned while talking through the bathroom window since I found it hard to leave the john long enough to unlock the door.

"We have to do it tomorrow night while she is asleep," I groaned through my crap pains.

"Okay. We have what we need, right? We just need to make sure that no one saves her fat ass. But wait. How are you going to explain to the police that you were not there with her?" I smiled for I had thought that through.

"When the fire trucks show up, I'll come walking down the road with a milkshake from McDonald's, saying that she was having cravings and made me go out and get some!" Kiki stepped up on the old shopping cart outside of the window and gave me a peck on the lips.

"My baby is a genius sometimes." The comment felt good. It was about time that someone complimented my brains.

The next night when Tina got home, I pretended to be asleep on the couch. (She usually got in around four since the strip club closed at three, and she liked to do the last dance since the guys were wasted by then and usually gave her more money.) I listened to her get ready for bed and close the bedroom door before I got up and tiptoed out of the trailer over to Kiki's. We'd already placed the gas in jars around the trailer to help get the flames going, and I even soaked the couch with some more before I left. All we had to do was douse the outside, jam the front door shut, and light her up. I have to admit, I was pretty excited as we poured the gas on the outside of the tin walls. Kiki was so into it that she tried to talk me into having a quickie behind the trailer before we lit her up, but my stomach was still aching so I declined and said after.

With a bit more gas in my tank, I wanted to cover the outside of her window a bit more and headed down there to do it. When my can was empty I hunched over in pain. I had to shit again.

"Kiki" I whispered softly as I could.

"Kiki, I have to go to the can. Wait to light it up 'til I get back." It was dark, but I could see her give me a thumbs-up. I hardly made it back inside to the can before the ooze shot out of me once again. It was a horrible feeling. Finishing up, I smelled something. I thought maybe I had gotten some crap on my hands like earlier, but after I sniffed them I realized it was a much stronger smell. Stepping out of the bathroom I was hit in the face with a wall of heat. The trailer was already going up in flames! She hadn't waited for me! I couldn't believe it.

Fast as I could, I sprinted for the front door. It was already sealed tight! I was screwed. By the time I made it back to the bathroom, the fire was inside of the trailer and eating away at the couch. I shut the bathroom door and threw a towel under the crack to keep the smoke out (a trick I learned when I used to be able to afford pot, though we used it to keep the smoke in). I had to keep far away from the door. If I didn't, I'd get blown up. I had left a dozen jars of gas through the whole place, four of which were under Tina's bed. And, to be honest, I was surprised that she wasn't awake and screaming at that point. Though I can't say that I was really too worried about her right then.

Opening the window, I yelled for Kiki. The plan required me to sprint to the McDonald's as soon as the fire started and for her to watch from behind a tree a few yards away to make sure Tina didn't get out. We didn't want to risk not killing her.

"KIKI! Help! I'm still in the trailer!" I stuck my head out of the window as far as I could, but it being a bathroom window on a thirty-year-old trailer, it was dang small.

"Baby! What are you doing in there!?" Kiki screamed at me as she raced over to me.

"I told you to wait, that I had to go to the bathroom."

"I thought you said you finished your can and to light it up…Oh, my God. We have to get you out of there."

"No shit!" I said as four successive explosions went off behind me. One of which half broke the door in.

"What should I do?"

"Go knock the bar off the front door and I'll have to make a run for it through the trailer!" She disappeared and came back quickly. By now, our neighbors had started to come out of their own trailers.

"Ok, it's off. Be careful." Again, she jumped up and gave me a kiss.

"I love you, Kiki. I'll make it out…for you!" With that, I turned around and ran out the bathroom door. At that point, I didn't even have to bother opening it—it was pretty much burned down. There were so many flames that I couldn't even see where I was going. Luckily, I didn't need to since I knew the path by memory. My parachute pants melted on my legs before I even reached the kitchen. And, just then, one of the glass jars exploded, sending shards of glass into my right side and splattered across my face. It felt like flaming fire ants were biting me everywhere. But somehow—I like to think it was sheer determination of love—I made it out of that trailer.

My neighbor, Al, sprayed me down with his garden

hose. It felt good and I didn't want him to stop. Mrs. Cummings, another neighbor, asked where Tina was. For dramatic effect, I pointed at the trailer and cried. (The tears were from the pain but I tried to make them look like they were from worrying.) Though I was in bad shape, it had worked—besides, being burnt was a better alibi. Finally, Tina was dead and I could live my life with Kiki and the millions we had coming to us. I was happy. Then...

"Oh, my God! My trailer!" It took a few seconds for the comment to register, but when I turned my head around I knew I was going to see her standing right behind me.

"Baby bear! Are you all right?" I could only smile. Kiki was the one to ask how come she wasn't in the trailer.

"Well, when I got home, I realized I had forgotten my pre-natal vitamins at work and I hate starting the day without one, so I went back to get them!" Kiki and I exchanged glances that both accused the other of not checking that she was in the trailer when we came back from her place.

As the fire trucks and ambulances arrived, I realized what bad shape I was in. Over half of my body had second degree burns and countless glass shards stuck in me. Hearing that I was going to have to have skin grafts made me feel faint, and that was when Tina's water broke. We shared an ambulance to the hospital.

When I woke up in the burn unit, I could hardly

see, but I could tell my body was completely covered in gauze. And, strangely, it felt nice. They must have given me the good drugs. A few minutes after I was up, a hot as hell woman nurse came over to me. She looked like an angel. In fact, I think she was an angel. She was so beautiful as she smiled down at me and checked my eyes. I knew in that instant that I was meant to marry her. It was love at first sight. How was I going to tell Kiki? How was I going to tell Tina? Christ, I was probably a dad by now.

"Finally awake, are you?" Her voice was amazing as well. I nodded.

"Well, let me be the first one to congratulate you! You're a father...it's a baby girl! The doctor told me I could bring her in to show you when you woke up. So sit tight, I'll be right back."

A girl? I knew Tina was wrong thinking it was a boy! A girl though...huh? Daddy's little girl? Maybe being a dad wouldn't be that bad. I was a stand-up guy. I could be a good father. Hell, maybe the hot nurse lady would raise her with me.

A few minutes into my dreaming of the nurse angel, I heard her voice as she walked into the room, though I couldn't lift my head to see her.

"Here she is! Your baby girl!" Then the nurse held the most beautiful little...*black* baby I had ever seen in front of my face. I couldn't help but cry. It wasn't mine. All this and it wasn't mine. I was free!

An hour after this realization, I was on cloud nine. I could leave Tina now, and when Kiki showed up, I was going to tell her I was leaving her, too. All this pain and suffering I had gone through, it was her fault. I was a fool earlier thinking I could be a dad and that Kiki was the one for me. Hell, maybe all of this happened for a reason. That dude God works in odd ways—maybe he just needed this to happen so I'd meet that angel nurse and marry her. Once I got out of this place, Nurse Angel and I would be together. Things were looking up; they were right for the first time in ages.

Kiki showed up and I was ready to give her the news. I was a new man now. No pussyfooting around. I was going to just tell her straight out.

"Honey. The doctor told me all about your injuries. I'm so sorry. But can you believe the kid's not yours?! We can be together now!"

"Speaking of that, I have something I have to tell you," I coughed out through my smoke-scarred lungs.

"Okay. But me first. I have some exciting news! Ricky, honey…I'm pregnant!"

A MODERN DAY ROMANCE

Niceeyes745,

Just saw your profile online. I must say, I think you sound very interesting! So I figured I'd give this a shot and send you an email to introduce myself. My name is John, I'm a chef and live in the city as well. What part do you live in? I live mid-town. So what do you do for work? Well, don't want to ramble on, so I guess this is enough to say hello! If you want to talk more just shoot me an email. I'm online a lot during the day.

Hope to hear from you!
PS-I love your smile…hehe
John
Aka-CuteChef77, haha

****

Hey CuteChef!

Thanks for emailing me! So nice to hear from a guy who doesn't start off an email with "nice boobs" or something much more vulgar! That is fantastic that you are a chef. Especially since I can't cook to save my life, haha. So I looked at your profile, you sound pretty cool yourself. I love Guns N' Roses too!

144

Ok, so let's see, to answer your questions… I live on the Upper East Side. Love it there! As for work, I work in an office for an insurance company. Basically boring data entry stuff, but it pays well and I can surf online all day! So I'm not complaining (too much, hehe).

So why don't you have a picture up on your profile? You really should. Truthfully, I usually won't email anyone without one. You know, to be safe, in case they aren't who they say they are (had a horrible experience once, went on a date with a guy who said he was 31, he showed up and had to be over 50!).

Well, better pretend I'm doing some work! But write me back and tell me more about yourself. I'll be here all day. Thanks for writing!
Joan

****

Joan!
Wow! I can't believe you wrote back so quick. I didn't even send that ten minutes ago. I must say I'm happy you did, thank you!

Yeah, I like the Upper East Side myself, though where I live is nice and close to the restaurant I work at so I don't have to take the subway.

As for my picture, to tell you the truth I'm not too computer-savvy, for one thing. And for another I used to be a model and hated women always coming on to me because of my looks and not my personality. I know that sounds like a line, but it is true. I'd rather have a woman read my profile and find it interesting than just click and look at pictures. I'll try to send you one later though, so you can see what I look like, since you passed the first test! Haha.

So a little about me? Hmmm… Alright, a super-short life summary! I grew up in Massachusetts, normal childhood. Got a modeling contract when I was eighteen so I moved to the city. Modeled for a while, but hated the vain culture. So I went to cooking school at night down in Union Square. Started working as a cook and worked my way around the city in various restaurants. Now I run one on Restaurant Row, been there for three years. Wow, is it sad that my life can be summed up in a few sentences?

Alright, here are a few ridiculously corny "get to know you" questions. My answers are on the right…

1-What is your favorite color?   -Brown
2-What is your favorite food?   -Smoked Salmon
3-Do you have any pets?   -Nope
4-How long have you been in the city?
        -Already answered that!
5-What do you look for in a man?
        -I look for nothing! Hehe
6-What are you going to be for Halloween?
        -Not sure yet

Alright, six should be good for now!   Well, looking forward to hearing from you!

John

＊＊＊＊

John,
Wow back at ya! You write back fast too! Good questions (for the third grade! JK!).

Answers-
1-Green
2-Sushi
3-Cat (named Carrie after the *Sex in the City* character! She is yellow.)
4-Seven years, came here for school and stayed.
5-Kindness and a sense of humor over anything.
6-So far I'm leaning towards Tigger! Always loved him!

Now for my life story…which will be even shorter! Grew up in Georgia—yes, I still have a bit of an accent. Haha. Same as you, normal life. I was an only child so I was a bit spoiled. ;). I moved to the city to go to school, got a degree in mathematics. Strange, I know. Funny how I don't even use my degree, a monkey could do this job for goodness sake! And I stayed in the city ever since then, and now I'm writing to you. End of story!

A model, huh? I must say now I am dying to see your picture! I feel a bit inadequate now. The closest I ever came to modeling was wearing an Easter Bunny suit for five dollars an hour when I was a teenager! So tell me this, you must be good-looking and you have a good job, so why are you on a dating website? And since you'll ask the same question back- I'm on it because I'm sick of all the pigs I meet in the bars and want to get to know someone before meeting them. You know? In truth, I feel like I already know you more than I have known my last two boyfriends!

Ok, questions for you:
1-Do you have any siblings?   -None
2-When was your last GF?
         -BF for me, three months ago.
3-Why did it fail?   -He was a loser.
4-What do you look for in a woman?   -N/A
5-SEND ME A PICTURE!   -hahaha

Looking forward to your next email!

Joan

****

Hey girl,

Got to love a woman with an accent! Good answers, by the way (though I'm not sure about Tigger, was never a big Winnie the Pooh fan...haha). I'm having fun with this, and it's only been a few hours! I know this might sound corny but I feel like we're making a connection here. Is that possible over the Internet? I mean, I'm getting all excited when I see the new email in my box! Alright, that isn't too manly...

Don't feel inadequate, from what I can tell in your picture you are beautiful. And you have ten times more of a brain than half the girls I have ever dated. Truthfully, this is probably the best relationship I have had in years! Heck by the time we meet, it'll be like we've been going out for years! Speaking of meeting, I don't know if this is too forward, but what are you doing for Halloween? I know it's only a few days away, but I don't have plans yet and was thinking of going to the Village Halloween Parade. I love that thing! If it's too early to meet though, don't worry. I'm fine with waiting until whenever you want, even if it's a long time.

Answers!
1-Two older brothers, both married and with kids…sigh.
2-Probably two months ago, if she counts.
3-Scheduling problems. Didn't have enough time to see each other.
4-Brains and a beautiful smile.
5-I will in the next email, I have to scan one into my computer, and who knows how long that'll take!

Alright, your only question this time…what do you want to happen in your future?

TTYL Cutie!
John

****

Why hello there Fabio! Haha

Thank you for the compliments! I must say I'm feeling that tingling sensation when I get emails from you as well. I have a good feeling about this! I actually don't have plans for Halloween yet, so let's make some! As long as you don't mind me being dressed up as a big orange Tigger! Haha... I'm excited! I feel like a little schoolgirl.

To answer your tough question: I see myself married, happily, with two kids in a big house outside of the city. Though, not too far away. Other than that, not much matters. Now you have to tell me yours, hope it's similar!

Well this is a short one, but the faster I send it to you the sooner I'll get to see what you look like!

XOXO
Joan

****

Beautiful,
I got my first kiss and hug and haven't even met you yet! This really is the best relationship I have had in years! Haha.
Now, I'm not lying to you about this, but your future plans...exactly the same as mine! I want to have a house outside of the city but close enough to go in to work in my own restaurant. The deal-breaker though...I want boys. What about you? I'll keep my fingers crossed!

Well, as you probably have noticed, I attached two

pictures of me. They are new, only a month or so old. One is of me in my chef's outfit behind the line and the other is me at Dave and Buster's hamming it up! I look horrible in them, but they are the newest ones I have. Hope you like them.

Well, I'll make this one short as well. Have to go drop off my laundry but I'll be right back to check your response!

****

Joan,
Well, I'm back from the laundry. Haven't gotten an email from you yet. You must be out to lunch or something. Wow, look at me, the worried boyfriend already! Alright, ignore this email!

Looking forward to hearing from you.
John

****

Gorgeous,
Hey, where did you go? It's almost five so I assume you got busy at work and couldn't get back to me. Just wanted to let you know I'm off to the restaurant for the night. I'll check my email when I get home and send you one in the morning.

Have a great night. Sweet dreams, my sweet!
John

****

Joan?

Hey, never got an email from you last night and it's almost noon today. I'm a bit worried that you're not getting my emails or something is wrong. I hope you're alright. Just email me when you get a chance so I know you're fine.

John

****

Missing Girl!!!

Ok it's now been two days and I haven't heard from you. We are supposed to make plans for Halloween, it's two days away! What is going on? I wish I got your number earlier so I could have gotten in touch with you.

I'm officially nervous. Have you been getting these? Did you get the pictures I sent?

Hope to hear from you.

John

****

Gulp,

Alright, I'm starting to get a bit worried that you saw my pictures and freaked out, I know I have gained a bit of weight since I modeled, but the face is the same! Just a bit chubbier. Well, if that is what it is, you can be honest with me. I can take it. Just, please contact me, I'm scared that

152

I already lost you, before I ever even had you…sigh

John

****

John,
Hey, I'm really sorry I haven't gotten back to you. Got crazy busy at work. But I do have some bad news. And I swear that it has nothing to do with your pictures. You're handsome. Anyway, I'm really sorry, but my ex-boyfriend and I are going to try and work things out. I do wish the best of luck to you though. You seem like a great guy. I know you'll find someone that will treat you great.

Best Wishes,
Joan

****

Joan,
Well, I must say I am crushed! I really thought we had a connection. I thought what we had was wonderful, it was rare to come across that. We worked so well together. And you did say he was a loser. He just better treat you right, if he doesn't you let me know! Haha. But seriously, if it doesn't work out with him, I'll be here. You got my email address, just shoot me a line anytime.

Miss you already!
John

****

Joan,
Hey there stranger. Haven't emailed you in a few weeks. Thought I'd check on you see how things are going with you and the BF.

Oh and I saw that your profile is still up on the dating site. Just thought you should know, don't want your boyfriend getting mad that you have an ad up!

Hope to hear from you.
John

DOODY DUTY

Ever step in dog shit? It ruins your whole day, right? On the occasions when you actually notice you stepped in it, you spend twenty minutes scraping your shoe on a curb, then you go into work and people start sniffing and looking around. You say it's you and they give you a disgusted look like it was you who shit. Then you spend thirty minutes in the bathroom with a pencil trying to scrape it out in the sink and rinse it off so you don't smell before your presentation to your boss. Of course, if you're like me, you slip while balancing on one foot, grab the faucet for balance, rip it off, fall on the floor, and get completely soaked. Leaving no time to get changed before your big chance to impress the bosses. Then your boss sees you before you go in front of the client, chastises you, and has your partner go in and do the presentation instead. You get pissed, start an argument, and get fired. All because someone didn't pick up their goddamn dog shit.

I was unemployed. All because of some ass who was too lazy pick up after his dog. After two weeks, I still hadn't found a job. My chances of ever finding one at that salary again were slim. And if I had had the chance to make my pitch, I would have gotten a bonus and pay raise

155

and a new office. Instead, I was sitting in my apartment with my savings running out, contemplating taking a job at Wal-Mart to pay the bills. Life was great.

I started to become a little obsessed with dog shit. I sat for hours looking out the window, watching all the people walk their dogs. There were at least ten in the complex—that I saw, anyway. And I started to notice a trend: almost no one was picking up after them. If I just knew whose dog had made the mess I stepped in I'd, I would... I'd never find out, because none of them picked up the crap; it could be any of them that ruined my life. They all deserved to pay for their laziness. Hell, it was against the complex policy not to pick up after your dog; it was even against the law in the town. Watching a black Pomeranian poop, I knew I had to do something about it.

After a quick run to the store, I was ready. Rubber gloves, paper bags, and a lighter. Everything I needed. Then it was a waiting game. It wouldn't be long, though. The dogs seem to crap every half hour. After merely twenty minutes, my first suspect came into view. A young girl in hospital scrubs walking her tiny little mutt, probably some expensive foofoo dog; I didn't get how something so small could excrete so much. I watched her from my second floor window as she made her walk around the courtyard—then, bingo. The little bastard squatted, pushed, and plopped out four long logs on the grass, not even three inches from the sidewalk. Did she pick it up? Ha! Of course not! She didn't even glance at it. It was time to put things into motion.

I had to sprint down the stairs to follow her, yet act casual at the same time. Since I didn't have a dog to walk, I pretended to talk on the phone, just taking a casual walk. She didn't even seem to notice me and I didn't have to follow too close to see that she lived on the first floor, which made my plan easier. Getting the apartment number, I ran back to my place, got the gloves and bag, ran down, and scooped up the foul pile into the bag. I had to wait until later for part two of my plan.

Unlike a lot of rebellious teens, I never did the flaming bag of poo gag. At almost forty, this was all new to me, but I couldn't imagine it being too hard. Put the bag down, light it, and run. Piece of cake, right? After dusk, I scurried over to her place, set the bag down, looked around, and lit it. Then, with a quick knock, I ran down the breezeway and around the corner. I got far enough away in time to be able to watch the show. My cover was that a man wearing a suit and talking on a cell would have nothing to do with a childish prank. If only they knew. Holding my phone to my ear, I watched as the door cautiously opened—though, unlike in the movies, she didn't start to stomp on it. Instead she closed the door, came back a minute later and poured water on it, and shut the door again. I was disappointed, to say the least.

I tried this three more times with different people. Some got madder than others, but no one stomped on the bags and I saw the same people not picking up after their dogs the next day. It was clear that I needed to do more to teach them a lesson. A note would do. A simple, nice note asking them to clean up after their dogs, only I'd write the note with their dog's own shit on their door—that might get their attention.

The first time I did it, I almost threw up. The smell was awful, and feeling the goo in my hands (even if I did have gloves on) was almost too much to take. But I got the job done nonetheless. Big, slimy brown letters spelling out *Pick Up After Your Dog*. I wanted to wait to see their reactions (I did it to four people the first night), so I took a nap and woke up around five a.m. to wait for them to leave for work. I could see two of the doors from my window, so I sat on a stool and got my binoculars out. It took almost a full two hours for the first person to come out. My back was killing me by then, but it was worth it. Through the round vision of my binoculars, I saw that the man didn't notice the note until he turned around to lock the door. It was hysterical. He jumped back as if it would attack him, then threw a fit. I couldn't hear him, but I'm pretty sure I knew what half the words coming out of his mouth were.

The next one came out only a few minutes later, a lady in her bathrobe taking her dog out to leave another shit in the grass. She didn't notice the note until she came back. It was amazing; she, too, backed away from it as if it might bite. She picked up her dog, started to cry, and raced away—I'm guessing to the office, for one of the maintenance men came back with her a few minutes later. He seemed to laugh at first, then they argued. I was hoping because he was telling her it wasn't his job to clean up her door. After a while, a bored-looking cop showed up and the lady yelled at him, too. After things calmed down, I took another nap, happy for the first time since I lost my job.

Over the next week, I did this seven more times. Though each time was getting more stressful, since people were on the lookout for the "Doody Bandit." Flyers started showing up on everyone's doors. It seemed I was starting a war! There were pink flyers asking everyone to be vigilant about keeping an eye out for this horrible defacer. Then there were green ones praising the bandit for getting people to finally clean up after their dogs. Then, of course, the complex issued a statement reinforcing the rules of picking up after your dog, that anyone found not doing this would be fined immediately. It also mentioned that anyone caught "defacing" the apartments would also face charges. My efforts were paying off.

The only problem was, now that everyone was in such an uproar, I couldn't do my duty. Only a few people, the ones trying to spite everyone, left their dogs' shit behind. There were people who staked out the piles of poo like they were money drops for some ransom. One balcony had a camera set up, focused on a pile. Another lady sat with binoculars, refusing to look away from another heap. It was comical, yet frustrating, that I couldn't continue. I settled down for five days. Slowly the cameras disappeared, the flyers stopped coming, and I figured I could go back to my mission. It had been days since I had looked for a job, but I figured this was more important.

Once again, I watched from my window. I saw a man, whom I had already gotten once, leave poop behind again. It was perfect; that way I didn't have to follow him. Instead, I could wait until the wee hours of the morning and do it again. This time, I planned on coating the door handle so he wouldn't have a way in without touching it. That should teach him.

At one in the morning, I snuck down, scooped up the poo, and raced to the man's door across the courtyard. Silently as I could, I started to write the words. It was then that I felt it on the back of my neck—something warm, slimy, and smelly hit me. Startled, I spun around to find four people trying to surround me, all wearing gloves, holding bags of poo. I knew I was in trouble. I only had enough ammo for one or two good defensive throws. They, on the other hand, had heaping bags full; they must have been saving up. Slowly, without saying a word, I snuck my hand in my bag, scooped up a handful, and pulled it out.

"Hold it right there, tough guy. You fire at us, one of us might go down, but you'll never make it out of here clean." The eldest of the group grunted as he cocked his arm back, ready to sling at me.

"We don't want any trouble, we want this to end. We want our dogs to be able to shit in peace without having our doors decorated the next day!" a little old lady yelled while scooping dripping poo from a knitted bag. I was about to scream at them, to tell them that one of their precious bastards lost me my job, but no words came out; instead, I snapped. Without thinking, I slung my shit at the leader, who ducked and launched his pile at me. It was a direct hit on the side of my face. I tried to make a break for it, but they were too prepared; it was a setup. Within seconds, I was in a fetal position trying to protect myself from the barrage of shit. I had it in my ears, in my nose— and, even worse, my mouth. I started to throw up at one point, but they didn't stop. It kept coming until they were out of ammunition.

"Let this be a lesson to you, asshole. Try it again and it'll be much worse."

An hour, four showers, two bottles of Listerine, and ninety-four Q-tips later, I was sitting naked at my desk looking at my apartment. I had tried to make it in without much of a mess, but it was impossible. There were brown footprints from the door to the bathroom, smudges on the walls, and even the countertops had globs. My place smelled like...shit. Refusing to clean up the mess, I tried to figure out how quickly I could move with no money. I checked my email to try distracting myself. It was then that I saw the message from my old boss, which I got yesterday but was too busy planning my attack to notice. Opening it, I sighed, wondering if he just wanted some files. It read:

Jack!

For crying out loud, why didn't you tell me you stepped in dog shit that morning?

Clare finally told me the whole story about how the sink broke because you were trying to make sure the smell was gone for the client. I know what it's like to
step in shit, both literally and figuratively. It screws up your day, I went overboard firing you. Your proposal went through with flying colors, you got that office you wanted. Yes, we want you back here on Monday (I left you two messages but you never called back), just try not to step in any shit on the way!

Suddenly, the smell and mess in my apartment didn't seem that bad. I even whistled while I cleaned it all up. That night I slept well, even if I did have a residual smell in my nose, for I had my job back and in two days I was going to go back to my normal life. As I fell asleep I even thought about apologizing to the dog idiots. Maybe I *had* gone a bit overboard.

Monday came quickly; I didn't really leave my apartment that weekend. I had take-out food and worked on files on my computer to make sure I was caught up on work. That morning I got up early, shaved, and put on my best suit and extra cologne. I was ready to reclaim the life I had. When I opened my door, I closed my eyes and took a deep breath, pleased at what a wonderful day it was. That was the exact moment when a warm, all-too-familiar taste filled my mouth.

"Get him!" I heard someone scream. Sadly, I couldn't open my eyes because of the shit that had hit my face. As I fell to my knees, hacked out the goo, and tried to wipe my eyes, I felt the plops hit me once again. Then, I heard something that made cry in fear.

"The apartment, the door is open! Destroy it!" I heard several sets of feet stomp by me as I tried so hard to get the mess out of all of my orifices.

By the time I stumbled into my kitchen and sprayed enough water on my face so I could see, my apartment had been ruined. There wasn't one item that didn't have some sort of brownish goo on it. It was horrible. I trudged over to the still-open door and saw the words *Leave Our Complex* smeared on it. Looking down, I saw my briefcase open with a nice big pile inside of it. They even managed to get some poo on each one of the suits in my closet, so even if I wanted to try to get the office, I wouldn't have been able to. I didn't make it to work that day; I stayed in a hotel that night and, a week later, I moved out of my apartment, though I took nothing with me. I found out later that there was a copycat. Someone left more messages on doors, and they assumed it was me.

For a long time I thought of ideas for revenge, of doing the same to all the apartments that did it to me. Then, I slowly realized dealing with all that shit had given me a high tolerance to it. It was that epiphany that made me realize that this all happened for a reason. The incident got me to start my own business: *Doody Duty Incorporated!*

That is the story of how my empire began. It started off as a dog-walking business, but then it grew into a dog feces removal business. We go to parks, complexes, and businesses to clean up after people who are too lazy to pick up their dogs' business. The concept caught on, so we started to add other services—stain and smell removal and our own line of clean-up products. Today we do business in thirty-six states and our products are for sale in forty-seven states. Stepping in shit sucks—take it from me, I know. That is why my company slogan is "Don't Step in It Again!"

TOOTH FAIRY INFLATION

"Mom, Dad! It came out, it just came right out, I didn't even wiggle it!" Jill screamed, running up to her parents holding the tiny tooth. Jay put down his coffee to look at his daughter's tooth. He picked it up, squinted at it, and held it to the light.

"Congratulations, honey, your first tooth!" Jill beamed and smiled wide to show the missing gap in her mouth.

"I bet you can't wait to leave it for the tooth fairy. You know she'll leave you money!" Carol said, leaning down to look at her daughter's mouth.

"I know! I'm going to be rich. You know, Terra at school said she got a hundred dollars for her tooth. I can buy so many Barbie's with that." Carol and Jay exchanged worried glances. Jay gave eyes that told Carol she'd better speak up.

"Well, honey, usually the fairy only leaves you a few dollars. Not a hundred—that tooth must have been really special." Carol realized as soon as the words were out of her mouth that she had phrased it wrong. Jill's small face scrunched up. She looked at her tooth, and frowned.

"You mean my tooth is not...special?"

Jay rubbed his face and took a shot at it. "No, no baby, it certainly is, especially since it is the first one you lost. What Mommy meant was that… a hundred dollars is not something the tooth fairy usually leaves. When I was a kid I only got a quarter!" Jill's face scrunched up in thought.

"Well, we'll just see what she brings tonight." With that, Jill turned and ran down the hallway. Jay and Carol looked at each other and rolled their eyes.

Later that night, Jill refused to put the tooth in a bag like her mother and father asked her to. She said the tooth had to come in contact with the pillow—that was how the fairy got called, something else that Terra had told her. As Jay and Carol kissed their daughter goodnight, Jill kicked her legs with excitement.

"I bet you the tooth fairy is so beautiful! I'm going to stay up all night to wait and talk to her. Maybe she'll even let me play with her wand."

Jay took this one. "Honey, don't you know, just like Santa, the tooth fairy won't come unless you go to bed. So you better fall asleep." Jill gave him a look of suspicion, but nodded when asked if she would try to sleep.

They left the door open a crack like they always did and then headed into the living room.

"How much are we going to give her?" Jay asked with pain on his face.

"Well, she is expecting a hundred, so we can't go and give her three dollars like I planned. I guess, twenty?"

Jay sighed. "That's not going to bode well for the budget. Especially once she starts losing them all, if we had to give her twenty a tooth…we'd go broke."

Carol nodded and looked a bit defeated. "Well, we'll give her five then and she'll have to get over it. I don't want her to be spoiled, anyway." The two agreed on the five, got it out of Jay's wallet, and watched television for an hour to make sure Jill was asleep before attempting anything.

Jill usually slept like a rock. There had been many times when they went in her room to watch her sleep or tuck her in, and she had never once stirred at their voices. They didn't want to take any chances, though, so they took off their shoes and tiptoed down the hallway. The plan was for Carol to switch the money for the tooth; her hands were smaller. Jay stood back to keep watch while Carol knelt down next to the bed. But, suddenly, she shot back as an ear-piercing scream came out of Jill. Jay flicked the light switch on to show his daughter that it was just Mom and Dad. Jay's gut tightened with guilt as his daughter's eyes filled with tears and she clenched her blanket.

"It's just us, baby, it's just us," Carol cooed. It took a minute, but Jill eased up and wiped the tears from her face.

"Why are you guys in here? You are going to scare the tooth fairy away!"

Jay sat on the edge of the bed and kissed Jill's forehead. "We were just coming to kiss you goodnight, that's all." Jay rubbed her back as he watched Carol squeeze the five tightly in her hand.

"Goodnight! Now go to sleep so you don't scare the tooth fairy away!" Carol said in a voice that was a bit too high-pitched. They both kissed her again and snuck out the door.

An hour later, the two were fighting to stay awake. They usually went to bed around nine, and it was already past ten.

"Ready to try again?" Carol asked Jay, whose eyes were half open. He nodded his head.

"Maybe only one of us should go in, though?" Jay suggested with a gravelly voice. Carol agreed. Jay waited outside the door while Carol crawled in on her knees. The idea of Jill losing her first tooth was very exciting, but the later it got, the less importance it held for him. After yawning three times, he watched Carol crawl back out. He was happy; they could finally go to sleep.

"All set?" Jay asked though another yawn. Helping Carol up, he saw the expression on her face. Now what?

"I can't find the tooth."

Jay rubbed his eyes, not wanting to deal with this; he had to work in the morning. "Well, just leave the five and if she finds the tooth, just say the fairy sometimes lets you keep your first tooth."

Carol looked back in the room then looked at the floor with an ashamed look. "That's not the only problem. When I was feeling around for the tooth, I accidentally pushed the five behind the bed."

Jay took a deep breath, trying to figure out the light side of the situation. "So we leave another five, then tomorrow we fish out the one that fell? No big deal." Jay walked to the kitchen and took his wallet out of the drawer. Rifling through, he saw that he only had two twenties. Putting down the wallet, he went to Carol's purse on the back of the door handle and fished through, only to find a stack of receipts where the money should be. Carol gave him a sheepish look as she entered the kitchen.

"I only have twenties. Crap, well, when she doesn't find the money, we can tell her that maybe it fell behind the bed. We'll lift it up and she'll find it? She might freak a bit at first, but when she finds it, she'll be fine." Carol hugged Jay as if to apologize.

"Let's get to bed." Jay walked with his arm around Carol down the hall. When they saw a light on in Jill's room they stopped, looked at each other, and peeked in.

"What's wrong, honey?" Jay asked in a whisper.

"I was just checking if she came yet. She hasn't, my tooth is still here."

Jay looked at Carol, who rolled her eyes. "Don't worry honey, she'll come…and if you are lucky, maybe she'll even leave your tooth for you to keep," Jay said, planting the seed for the morning.

"Dad! Don't be silly, she has to put the tooth into a machine, otherwise she won't get the money. She *has* to take the tooth, Terra said so."

Jay sighed and tried to talk his daughter out of her beliefs, but she wouldn't buy it; the tooth had to be taken. For the third time that night, he and Carol kissed their daughter good night.

Lying down on their bed, they fought to stay awake. Jay caught himself falling asleep twice, but the thought of disappointing his daughter kept startling him awake.

"Why don't we just set the alarm for an hour or two from now and we'll just sneak in, grab the tooth, and then in the morning we'll say to check behind the bed for the five?" Carol didn't answer him. Jay propped himself up on an elbow to see his wife sound asleep. Lying back down, he rubbed his eyes, trying to stay awake. Fifteen minutes, then he could try to get the...

The bright light woke Jay with a start. It was morning! He hadn't gotten the tooth. Ignoring Carol snoring beside him, he raced out of the bed and down to Jill's room. Her bed was empty. His heart sank. Lifting her pillow, he hoped to find the tooth, but it wasn't there. The room was too small for Jill to hide, so he calmly walked to the living room to see if she was there. She wasn't. The kitchen, not there either. The last place he thought to check was the bathroom. There she was. Standing on her little stool, leaning into the mirror. Jay didn't say anything as he watched her tiny hands work inside of her mouth. He took a deep sigh and built up some courage to speak.

"What are you doing honey?"

She turned toward him with floss hanging out of her mouth that was covered in toothpaste. She answered him with gurgles. "Putting my tooth back in. The tooth fairy didn't want it. It must have not been ready to come out." Jay's heart broke a little.

After a few hugs Jay got Jill's mouth washed up and the tooth out. He told her about how sometimes the tooth fairy gets so busy she can't get to everyone's house in one night, and that she would definitely come tonight.

Jay arrived home that night to find Jill bouncing around the house and Carol looking distraught. Jill ran over to him, hugged him, and ran away screeching with joy.

"What's...going on?"

Carol rolled her eyes and talked in a low voice. "Not only did she find the five dollars behind her bed, which she said must have been a down payment on her tooth—how she knows what a down payment is, I have no clue. Anyway, she said everyone in her class went on and on about how if the tooth fairy doesn't visit you the first night, she doubles the money the second night. She is now expecting two hundred dollars this evening."

Jay couldn't help but laugh. "Well, we can't leave money if we can't get the tooth from her!"

Carol didn't laugh. "Look, we leave another five dollars and she'll learn a good lesson about money."

"We do that and all the kids are going to tease her about how much she got."

"Then she'll learn a good lesson about not caring what others think." Carol got up and paced the kitchen.

"This sucks. Why couldn't I just get the tooth last night?"

"Don't worry, we'll get it tonight and things will be fine."

That night they decided to wait until Jill was asleep for a good two hours before attempting the exchange. This time, Jay was going to be the one to make the switch. Jay crawled in the room slowly, slid his hand under the pillow, and snagged the tooth. Pulling out his hand, he wanted to shout out with victory. With his other hand ready to slide the money under the pillow, his thumb accidentally caught the pillowcase, pulling it, jerking Jill's head sideways. Jill's eyes shot open and a scream once again came out. Jay pushed himself back, ready to run away, not wanting to get caught, when he realized he needed to calm Jill down.

"Baby, baby, it's just me. It's ok, it's ok, don't worry." Jill sat up, flipped on her Disney lamp, and looked under the pillow. When she saw the tooth was gone, she smiled big, but then realized there was no money. She looked at Jay and saw the five-dollar bill sticking out of his hand.

"You stole my money! Daddy, why are you stealing from me!" The tears burst out. Jay tried to take her in his arms, but she fought him off. Carol had to come in to settle Jill down. When the tears stopped, Jay tried to make up a story about how the tooth fairy gave him the money to give to Jill because she was in a hurry. Jill wouldn't buy it.

"I want my money back!" Jay handed her the five dollars, hoping she would relax.

"All of it Daddy. I'm not stupid, that is only five dollars. I want the rest of the hundred too! It was my tooth, it's my money." Carol gave Jay a look that said she didn't know what to do.

"Let me see if she left any more money, honey." Jay ran out to his wallet. It was payday and the wallet was filled with the money for the week. Money they needed for the groceries and other things. He pulled out the wad, peeled off two twenties, and went back to the room. Reluctantly, he handed it to Jill. She looked at the money, scowled.

"There should be more, Dad."

Jay buried his face in the blanket on the bed before

171

answering. "That is all there is, honey. The fairy said she might be able to give you more next time." Jill had on her pouty face, but she seemed to have accepted the situation.

"Well, I guess that is alright, because this tooth—" she poked her front tooth with her tongue and it wiggled a bit, "—is just about to come out. Probably tomorrow. I hope I get more money then."

Jay stood up, patted his daughter on the head, and walked out of the room dazed. Carol joined him in the kitchen five minutes later. Jay counted his money over and over again.

"There is no way we can afford another tooth at those prices."

Carol hugged him. "We'll figure it out."

The next morning, Terra showed up at the door to walk to the bus stop with Jill. Jay did his best to not yell at her for ruining their family budget. As the two walked away, he saw them talk back and forth. They looked over their shoulders and giggled as they waited at the corner by the house. Jay wondered what they were talking about.

"You were totally right, Ter! They fell for it. They thought I really was upset and gave me more and more money! I got fifty dollars!"

OBAMA WILL NOT SCARE ME

I guess there is time to tell you my story before we are called in. I'll tell you, I've been alive for sixty-five years and nothing has ever scared me more than Obama. Hell, I still have nightmares about him. For a while, I cringed when I saw him on television—his voice sent chills down my spine. The man darn near ruined my life; I could be dead because of him.

I guess it really ain't fair to blame Obama, though. It ain't his fault, ain't his fault at all. It's the stupid employees' fault, and if I knew which one…man, I would, well, I probably wouldn't do anything. Hell, it got me here! Anyway, I'm getting off track. I'm being rude. My apologies, here I am rambling and I haven't introduced myself or even explained why the President scares me so much. My name is Randolph Emerson, Randy to most. I'm the night janitor at Pine and Farm Architects' main offices. Well, I say night, though I'm the only janitor. I say night because I don't clean until after six when the employees leave. It's a great job, really—like I said, been at it over thirty years. I work alone, don't have to listen to a boss (he only leaves me sticky notes if he needs something done—other than that, I talk to the man twice a year). I even make my own hours. I come in when I want and take as long as I want, long as everything is cleaned before the morning. Though, having done it for so long, I have a pretty standard routine. Usually it varies only by an hour at most, and that is if they've had meetings and left food out. Basically, I come in around six, empty trash, dust, vacuum, and clean the bathrooms 'til I'm done, which is usually around midnight—it's five floors after all. I think that is about all you need to know about my job; if I think of something else, I'll throw it in.

Obama. I guess that is what I should talk about next. Now, I proudly voted for that man. Hell, I cried when he got elected. I was alone in the offices, cleaning, listening to the radio I keep on my trash cart. Each time he won a state, I hooted and hollered knowing no one was around to hear me. As the race got closer to finishing, I went into the kitchen, turned on the flat screen in there, and cleaned as I watched. By the time it was announced that he had won, I was glued to the television. When Obama came on to give his speech, I fell to my knees and wept. If my father were alive to see a black man like himself become president, man, I can't imagine what he would have done. The stories he used to tell me about segregation when he was a kid would make you sick. This story isn't about that, though.

Now you see, Obama was elected; everyone was happy, but nothing out of the ordinary happened. Then came Inauguration Day. When I arrived to clean, I knew instantly that they'd had a party. Cups and plates were stacked in every trashcan, balloons were in the hallway, and, worst of all, the usual million cake crumbs were strewn all over the carpets. Now, it's my job to clean up after their messes, so I don't complain much, but I do enjoy a normal day a lot more than any day with a party or meetings. Anyway, so I was cleaning, doing all the normal stuff—nothing out of the ordinary, really. I was in good mood since Obama was in office.

I guess before I tell you what happened, I should tell you about the security system in the offices. The place is locked up like Fort Knox. First of all, to get in, you have turn off the alarm with a code and a thumbprint; only a few employees have this privilege. When I'm cleaning, the alarm is actually on. I turn it off to enter, then put it back on while I clean (company rules). Basically, what I'm saying is that no one can get in the office when I'm there, except for a few of the bigwigs. Also, if I arrive and the alarm is on, I know no one is in the building. That night, the alarm was on. Oh, and besides this, every entrance to every floor has a keypad; you have to have the code to get into that floor. Basically, what I'm trying to tell you is that absolutely no one can get in the building when I'm cleaning.

You may be figuring out where I'm going here. Now, the night of the inauguration I was in a good mood. Hell, there were leftover cake and snacks all over the place, and I was having myself a party. As I hummed to myself, I walked into the kitchen, snapped on the lights, and saw a large black man standing in front of me. In thirty years, this has never happened to me. I have run into people working late, but they were never in a dark room like this fellow was. Seeing this person in front of me was such a fright that my heart slammed—so hard that I lost breath, felt pains down my arm, and collapsed. Gasping for air, I looked up to the man, figuring it was someone about to rob the place and kill me to get what he

wanted. It was then that I noticed he was wearing a suit. As the pain over took me, I noticed he wasn't moving. The pain in my chest forced me to close my eyes; when I opened them again, I was looking at President Obama. By the time I realized it was just a life-sized cutout for their inauguration
party, it was too late. I was having a heart attack.

Thankfully, it was only a mild attack, but I still had to go to the hospital—was laid up there for four days. Had to have my kids take care of the cleaning those nights. I didn't tell anyone it was because of Obama; I was a bit embarrassed that a piece of cardboard would give me a heart attack. I was ready to go back to work that next week. (Well, *I* was—my wife and doctor suggested another few weeks off.) It was good getting back to work, even if my breathing was a bit off and I was a tad jumpy. When I entered the lunchroom that first day back I closed my eyes, flicked on the light, and told myself that the cutout was going to be there in front of me. It was not. I sighed with relief and started to clean.

By the time I got to the fifth floor, I had found my groove and was feeling pretty good, even if my wife called nine times to check on me. Then I entered the IT offices. As I flicked on the lights, bam! It happened again. There was Obama. Though my heart slammed, I knew I wasn't having a heart attack. I did, however, have to sit down for a solid forty minutes before I stopped shaking. I was again embarrassed—humiliated, really. There I was, a man in his sixties, getting the crap scared out of him by a piece of cardboard. When I came home later than usual that night, my wife asked if everything went
alright. I lied and said I was fine.

That night was when the nightmares started. They were weird, to say the least. I just remember being chased by Obama through a garbage dump. When he caught me, he stuffed about five pounds of cake in my throat. I'd always wake up gasping. When I saw Obama on the morning news, it sent shivers down my spine. That night at work, I was ready for the cutout in the IT room. I figured that was where they had placed it permanently. So as I was four offices away, I started to psych myself up for it so, when I entered, I would be ready for it. It didn't work, though, because when I entered the office three doors down, there he was. And not just standing there, oh no. This particular room was cut in half by cubicle walls, so I didn't see him until I rounded the second cubicle. And not only was he not just standing, someone had put a winter hat and a long wool trench coat on him, making the cutout seem even more real. This time, I hit the floor again.

As I lay on the carpet, looking up behind me to see Obama, I laughed and cried. It was ridiculous. A piece of cardboard was going to end up killing me! My chest ached, my arms tingled; it was a horrible feeling and I could only imagine what I was doing to the heart I was supposed to be resting. Now, I don't want to bore you with the same story over and over again, so to sum things up, this happened EVERY night that week. Each night it was in a different room, different clothing on it, and I was just a pile of goo. By Friday, I was trembling just entering the building. I kept telling myself over and over again that Obama would not scare me, that it was just a stupid cutout—yet, every time, bam! It was a nightmare.

I wanted to destroy the thing, to shred it up and

throw it in the dumpster, but I had never stolen or destroyed one thing in those offices in thirty years and I didn't plan to now. I wasn't going to lose my job because of a cutout. Nor was I going to tell anyone that it scared me. I ain't no pansy; at least, I don't want anyone thinking that. Anyway, the point is, if the thing stayed in one place, I would have been fine. But for some stupid reason they passed the thing around, taking turns keeping it in offices, dressing it up. They even hid it a few times where it would scare people, on purpose. Around corners, peeking out from the behind the vending machine, in a bathroom stall. I swear, the heart is an amazing muscle; the fact that my heart was still working is proof of that.

About two weeks after constant startles, of being terrified of seeing any sort of image of Obama, I looked like a drug addict. I had bags under my bloodshot eyes from not sleeping well, and I was losing weight (which wasn't a bad thing). My wife was concerned, made me go to the doctor, and I still didn't tell anyone what was going on. It was getting to a ridiculous point. My cleaning was taking me an extra two hours a night because I would walk slowly, creep into each room, and pop the light on until I found the cutout so I could relax and clean the rest of the place. I was getting used to it by week three. It just sucked how much time it added to my nights, having to sneak around 'til I found Obama. Then one night, something different happened.

The sun was down. I was sneaking into each room, looking for Obama, praying he wouldn't scare me again. Things were going pretty smoothly; then I entered the president's office. Now, I had yet to see Obama in there and figured he wouldn't be. The man who ran this place would let his employees have fun, but wouldn't do it himself, I thought. I flicked the light on and saw the figure in the back corner, his back to me. *Shit*, I muttered to myself. I was a bit disappointed that the president would have the President in his office, but I was happy at least to have found the cutout so I could speed my way through the rest of the rooms. I turned my back to the cutout and went for the trash. As I emptied it, I heard a rustling noise behind me. Now, I was scared of this cutout, but once I turned the light on and got over the sudden fright, it was just a cutout to me. Turning, more out of curiosity than of fear, I saw that it wasn't a cutout; it was actually a man.

The large man, who wasn't even black or wearing a suit, came rushing at me. Now, here is the funny thing: unlike all the other times when the fake Obama had given me heart attacks, I felt no fear at this man rushing me. Imagine that. Being that I was just inside the office door, I was able to back up, shut the door, and run before he reached me. As I ran down the hall, I could hear the door open behind me. I reached the alarm panel and hit the panic button, realizing that it might not have been the best of ideas. The panic button called the police; yet, at the same time, it sealed off all the office doors. No one could get in or out of each floor without the panic access code, which no one but the police and the president had. I was trapped on the floor with this man until the police arrived.

The one thing I had to my advantage was knowledge of the office layout and keys to every room. As I started to run down the hall, I looked over my shoulder to see the man trying to get out of the main door.

I was happy to know he was trying to get away and not kill me; only he was trapped in here now. His only way out was to be arrested or...to take me hostage. Realizing this, I snuck into the only office on that floor that had more than one exit. This one had a back door that led into a conference room and a side door that led into the next office. I crouched behind the desk, trying not to breath heavily. I immediately cursed myself when I realized I had left my cell phone on my cleaning cart.

"Get out here now, you fat ass, and let me out of this building!" The scream was pretty far away, but I could still hear the anger in the tone. I stayed still and didn't move.

"I'm not messing around here—if you don't come out in five seconds, I will find you and shoot your balls off." That did not sound too pleasant to me, but I decided to not move, anyway. Only problem was I could hear him flicking on lights and flipping desks. I had only a few minutes before he reached me. I was going to have to time my move just right so he didn't see me sneak out to the back conference room. When I heard him in the next office, I made my move and slipped out the back. It took everything I had to keep the scream in my mouth as I ran right into the Obama cutout. It had a baseball cap and a spring jacket on it. I was fighting back tears when I thought of a plan.

In the conference room window, there was a large crystal book with some etching saying it was an award for something. I didn't bother reading it at that moment. I grabbed it and Obama and headed for the conference room door. By this time, the intruder was two rooms past where I was. I grabbed the trash bag out of the can near the door and went back to grab one of the swivel chairs on wheels. I tore the bag so I had it in a nice long strip and then tied Obama to the chair so his feet were of the ground. I pushed the chair with my foot and Obama slid nicely. If the intruder looked just at the right moment, he would think it was me.

With the crystal book in my hand and my foot on the chair leg, I took a deep breath and then faked a loud cough. I waited until I heard the running footsteps and then shoved the chair. The second it started to roll into the hall, I darted back into the conference room and around to the office I was hiding in and out the door. It was then that I heard the five gunshots. It had worked perfectly; I was right behind the man and with one swing downward, I had knocked him out.

As I stood over the crumpled, unconscious man, I looked up to see the Obama cutout in front of me, five bullet holes in it, two in the head and three in the chest. The man would have killed me. Pissed at this thought, I let the glass book slip out of my hand onto his head. It landed with a wet *thunk* that turned my stomach a bit. I had never hit a man before, let alone with a glass book. Hearing the sirens outside, I quickly ran to the office door and put my hands on my head to show I was not a threat.

I was cuffed at first, but quickly released when the president of my company showed up. Wow, we are running out of time, better finish this story up. Anyway, I'm sure you saw it on the news, but the man was a terrorist. Before coming to the office he killed one of the executives, after he got codes to get in the building out of him. That is how he got in without me knowing. You see, my bosses are architects, but what I didn't tell you is that they have government contracts. They have built dozens of buildings and bases for military use. The man was trying to get the blueprints for a massive attack. To cover up the blueprints being gone, he was going to burn down the building. Come to find out, I saved a lot of people. My boss gave me early retirement and a bonus for my bravery. I also got so many gifts from people after the news talked it up, saying my efforts might have saved thousands. Silly, really—I was just doing my job.

Man, makes me laugh. Obama almost killed me, then saved my life. I mean, really, who would have thought?

"Ladies and gentlemen, it is time for all of you now to go on stage and take your seats. The Presidential Medal of Freedom ceremony is about to begin."

Guess it is time for us to go. I got to say, I'm a bit nervous. This Obama is not going to be made out of cardboard!

RUDOLPH,
THE LATER YEARS

Rudolph was drunk again. Santa sent the elves out to get him. Three came back with black eyes, and poor Dooley simply disappeared. Furious about having to miss the end of *CSI Boise*, Santa put on his coat in a foul mood. Tromping outside, he tried to calm himself by repeating over and over again, *I'm the JOLLY Saint Nick, JOLLY.* He didn't have to look far for his rouge-nosed animal; the glowing red light coming from the barn was a dead giveaway. As he approached the glimmer, he could hear slurred singing: "Me, the red-nosed reindeer. I have a very shiny nose." Coming from behind the pine trees. With a deep breath, Santa confronted his former team leader, who was making snow angels.

"Rudolph, with your nose so bright, what the hell are you doing out here tonight?"

After a quick hiccup and a low rumble of a burp, the buck replied, "Waiting for Mrs. Claus to jingle my bells." Santa couldn't take it when Rudolph referenced the affair he was having with his wife. They swore it was over, but he was always suspicious. After their romance, Santa had demoted Rudolph from lead reindeer to taillight; Rudolph had been drinking ever since. This was the third time

Santa had to round him up after a binge. Having had enough, Santa grabbed a hoof and started to drag Rudolph back to the barn.

"That's the last time I let you join in any reindeer drinking games!" Santa growled. Rudolph kicked the hand off of his hoof and stood up.

"Where is that ho, ho, ho, anyway?"

"I'd like to stuff your stocking, you—" Santa barked.

"What, with that bowlful of jelly?"

Giving up, Santa left Rudolph in the snow and headed back inside.

"It ain't my fault your roasted chestnuts don't do it for her anymore!" Rudolph yelled to his back.

Santa got back inside just in time to see the end credits of *CSI*. Chugging his eggnog, he tried to calm down. He had to tell himself that he couldn't do anything about Rudolph because the stupid buck was almost as big a celebrity as himself. *Stupid song, making him famous.* He didn't even need him anymore; he had halogen lights and GPS. His red nose was useless; he only let him sit on the back of the sleigh as a taillight because the missus begged him to not fire him after the affair. She said if he did, Rudolph could sue them. Damn unions.

As the nog started to soothe him, he heard a hissing noise by the window. Turning around, he saw yellow liquid splashing against the glass.

"That's it, Rudy! I'm going to deck your halls!" The stream finished with a couple more squirts as Santa grabbed his shotgun off the mantel and loaded it.

"It's going to be a blue Christmas without you,

Rudy!" he yelled as he ran out the door. Looking to his right, he saw Rudolph trying to gallop away and fly, but the reindeer was to drunk too get off the ground more than a few feet. Santa pulled the trigger; the shot missed and instead hit the North Pole, taking a good chunk out of it. The blast woke up the whole village; elves ran out from everywhere, and the other deer watched from the barn windows, not wanting to get involved.

A few elves tried valiantly to stop Santa from coming to town, but he merely kicked them out of his way. His second shot hit the silver bells; he could hear them ring, ring-a-ling.

"Ho, ho, HO!" Santa bellowed as his cheeks got rosy from the cold.

"Rudolph, with your nose so bright, won't you guide my shot tonight?" Santa sang to himself as he reloaded his gun and followed the tracks in the snow. The tracks led into the workshop; Santa followed them. Presents and toys for good girls and boys were everywhere. Santa readied his gun and looked around, knowing Rudolph couldn't cover his nose for long.

"Kristopher Kringle! You put that gun down right now!"

Santa ignored his wife, who appeared in the door behind him. "Stay out of this, woman!" he growled over his shoulder, just as the high-pitched, annoying squeal of Rudolph's nose blared in the distance. Santa focused his shot on the red glare that was starting and pulled the trigger. The light was instantly extinguished.

"Oh, holy night," Mrs. Claus whispered to herself.

The next day, Santa stubbornly watched Mrs. Claus

leave with her luggage. He didn't even try to stop her—four hundred years of marriage was enough for him. So what if she was going to move to the big city and finally take the offer to join the cast of the *Real Housewives of the North Pole*? Without her, he could finally let the jingle bells rock.

That night, drunk on eggnog, Santa enjoyed juicy venison burgers as he sang to himself, "Rudolph the red-nosed reindeer, tasted great with a glass of beer."

STAN THE MAN

Yes, I am Satan. So what?

Since, oh, the beginning of time, I've been given a bad reputation. It's not fair, but when you have been deemed the most evil being in the universe, what can you do? It's like in high school when a rumor is started about you. Even when it's not true, there are always people who will believe it, just because it was said. That is sort of my situation. Back when Ted (or God, as you know him) and I were best buds, we got in a fight. (Look, I knew him way before he got the "God" label. We called him Ted, and that is what I still call him. What is he going to do, damn me to hell?) He started some rumors, everyone believed him, and I got forced out of our plush little pad. Was I pissed? You better believe it. I tried for a few thousand years to get back up there, even admitting to my wrongdoing, which I did not actually do. The rest is history. Now, I am the leader of the underworld forever.

I'm sort of like your boss at work. Most likely, you hate his guts, but he is probably a good guy. He is just doing his job. That's what I do. I'm stuck with a job, so I do it. And, to tell the truth, I'm not that bad of a guy. I don't enjoy unleashing punishment on the souls that I obtain, but they deserve it, so I give out the orders for their damnation.

In case you're wondering as well, hell is not filled with fire and brimstone. Far from it. We actually remodeled in the mid-'80s (we do that every few hundred years when the budget allows—Ted is a cheap bastard). We have a gym, a Starbucks, cable TV, a casino, and even theater. It's sort of like a regular town. The only differences are that at night people don't get to sleep; they have to go into their "punishment beds" and receive whatever punishment they have been given. Not a big deal, really. Sort of like working out, it sucks at first—it's hard and makes you miserable, but after a while, you get used to it and it's not that bad.

Like anyone, I get bored with my job. I sit behind a desk and soul after soul comes in front of me. It's sort of like being a judge; my assistant reads me the case file, I let them plead their case, and I assign a punishment. It's monotonous. In the early 1700s, the work started to back up. Now, man, now we have a backlog of about a million and counting. All these souls stuck in a massive waiting room. It's this huge room that looks like a doctor's office. There are tons of water machines everywhere, but the catch? No bathrooms. You see, since this is hell, I'm forced to put in a certain amount of "punishments" a day. If I don't and I just happen to get audited, I get called into Ted's office and get chewed out. It's the same damn argument every time. I say, "Well, if you hadn't forced me out, I wouldn't be doing this." Then he comes back with,

"Oh, that again. Let it go, man!" Then I cross my arms and pout. Then he goes on about how his job is much harder, so I say, "Let's switch for day." He laughs, brings out a bottle of Satusa (like your vodka), and we both get drunk. Nothing gets resolved and I go back to work. This has been the routine for the past...long time.

In the 1800s, I found a way to go to Earth for visits. All I had to do was pick a recently deceased new member of our society's body. Using some old mumbo-jumbo magic stuff (I won't bore you with the details), I could put myself in their dead corpse. At first it was a bit awkward to get used to, like driving a new vehicle for the first time. But once you get the hang of it, no problem. The trick was to pick a body that had died of natural causes and was in good shape. One that got hit by a car, not too good to use. A young man who died of a drug overdose, perfect. No exterior damage.

The bodies wouldn't rot as long as I possessed them. There were still a few problems, though. For one, I had to make sure to get away from the town where I took the body, so no one would recognize it and freak out. Secondly, the body never grew old. So I could use it for as long as I wanted, but you stick around with people for a few years without changing a bit and they get suspicious.

The first time I took a body, I appointed a Russian serial killer named Vladimir to do my duties down below. (I admit it, a monkey could do the job.) The only part that sucked was I had to come back to hell every now and then to make an appearance so no one got too suspicious.

Which meant that when I did this, I had to find a place to hide the body I was using. As soon as I departed the body, it would start to decompose. I got away with it a few times, usually waiting 'til nighttime and hiding in the woods, then leaving the body. On the fourth visit, someone found the body I was using; when I entered it again, I was in a morgue so I had to start over. To do so, I had to go back to hell and wait for a good candidate. That is when I realized what Vladimir had done to my work.

The bastard was mean; he was making the place like, well, hell. He tried to get rid of Wednesday bingo and ice cream Fridays! The nerve of him. When I got to my office, the complaint box was filled to the brim. Feeling guilty, I went through every one of them, addressed them accordingly, and took back my job from Vladimir. He threw a fit and said that this place is not like hell should be. I told him not to believe everything he reads in books and hears at church. To punish him, I assigned him to work as one of his victim's butlers.

Ever since then, I have found a few people I trust well enough to run this place when I go on my trips. Ed Gein for one, hell of a man. Yeah, he might have cut off women's nipples and made necklaces out of them, but he is kind hearted and never once thought of getting rid of our monthly socials or setting the dance floor at Club Hell on fire. I can rely on him, probably because his mother is here as well and he knows if he messes up, she'll give him an earful.

By the mid-1900s, I was itching to follow my true passion, which I never dared tell anyone down her— singing and dancing! When I first started this job, there wasn't much singing and dancing on Earth—the little we did have was usually drunken grunts in bad rhythm along with stumbling around. Yet, I always enjoyed it. Then as it evolved, I kept my eye on it. The Romans started putting on shows. I loved the acting; it was amazing. Then the Italians started singing operas and, from there, it blossomed into a true art. I was enamored. Every day, while everyone went to their torture sessions, I went to my room (no, I don't get tortured—having to be the boss is torture enough) and watched Eartha-vision (like your TV, but I can see anything anywhere in the world at any time I want), searching the channels until I found a production of something, anything really.

I soaked it all in and then would try out numbers of my own. I would clear aside my ottoman and couch and dance around my room like a fool in love. Then I would turn on my stereo loud as I could (to drown out my voice) and sing my head off. Now, I'm not cocky, but I think I am pretty darn good. Especially when a very famous singer, whom I'll leave unnamed, came in front of my desk one day. He agreed to do "private" work for me at night. At first, he was a bit nervous that I was going to do something perverted to him. When he realized I wanted singing and dancing lessons, man, was he thrilled. We struck up a friendship, and as more singers and dancers made their way into my layer, we started up a dance troupe. Around that time, we put in the theater. It is called Beelzebub's Playhouse!

191

We put on a show every Thursday night. We take Fridays off and, the rest of the week, we rehearse a new show. Sometimes it's a variety show, and other weeks it's a musical or a play. It's great fun and, man, if you saw the names on the playbill, you'd faint. If this were on earth, the tickets would sell like hotcakes. Being hell, we are sold out every night, probably because I make it mandatory for everyone go.

Even with all the satisfaction I get out of this, I still want to make it on my own. You see, here they have to love me. Hell, I could take a dump on the stage and they would cheer and say it was amazing. Our resident critic would write a rave review in the paper: "Mr. Satan defecates with grace!" That is why I have decided to make a go of it. I have been looking for the right body for ages and, finally, I have found one. Twenty-three years old, in amazing shape, with a background in musical theater—so his body is perfect for this! Luckily for me, he had an enlarged heart and died while performing *Swan Lake* at his local theater in Iowa. You might ask why he went to hell. Well, he had some odd fetish of killing small animals and leaving them on people's doorsteps. Seems harmless, but a woman had a heart attack and died at the site of her cat cut in half.

John Wayne Gacy came to me about fourteen years ago. He became an assistant when Ed Gains decided to transfer and work at the bingo hall (he is the number caller now). John is a good worker, though he is a bit odd. The best part is, he couldn't believe he was here at first. He became a preacher in jail, thought that would get rid of his sins. Fool. Once the sin is made, there is no going back. That is why I have twice as many people as Ted does; the bastard is picky. Vain, too—won't take anyone unless they worship him like crazy. Me, I welcome everyone with open arms. Anyway, I'm getting off track here. With the body ready and John set to take my position over for a while (with strict rules that, if he tries to make anyone his boy-toy, he'll be sorry), I practiced my solo and danced for auditions until I was perfect.

When I first entered the body, I snuck out of the funeral home, found a new set of clothing on a line behind a beat-up old house, and hitchhiked four hours away. Once I was far enough away, sure enough I wouldn't be recognized, I opened up a portal and had my secretary (who is Mother Theresa, by the way, though everyone down here calls her Mama T) send me up a fake ID, credit card, and enough cash to get me through for a while. Yeah, I have some powers while on earth, but nothing too great. And certainly nothing that would help me get the lead role in a show, unless I wanted my competition to be eaten by a bear-sized sewer rat.

I booked a flight with my new ID of Stan Murphy (real original, I know, calling myself Stan—but, hey, I go by it down there as well) and arrived in New York City that night. It had been a century or so since I had been to the Big Apple, so I took a week to look for an apartment and sightsee. I had such a great time that I got really depressed that I couldn't live like this forever, that I couldn't be a normal human, that I was only going to get this one shot to live my dream. And if I made it, I'd only have a few years to enjoy it. And, really, what is a few years when you're immortal?

Getting over my depression, I saw every show on Broadway. I laughed, I cried, and I cheered out loud! I was in heaven—well, not literally. I hate heaven; they are so stuck-up and uptight. The place is boring as...it's boring. I mean, really, they don't even have ice cream nights.

Ready to start auditions, I went to Capizio's and bought several pairs of dance belts, shoes, and tights for auditions. Then I hit the newsstand, grabbed a *Backstage*, and read it at Tasti-Delight while I had my favorite chocolate and vanilla twist. Can you believe that stuff only has, like, ten calories? I made a note to add Tasti-Delight to our ice cream bar and went about reading the list of auditions. I didn't want to start small; I didn't have the time, really, so I circled the two listings for the big ones and crossed my fingers.

Usually, to get the big auditions for a major musical, I would need an agent and an amazing résumé. No problem. I brought back a super-agent from the eighties, gave him a new body, and put him in a fake office. Together, we made up a fake résumé that no one could dispute and he got me into both auditions! I was impressed by my own ingenuity.

Now, you would think I would be nervous messing around on earth, that God would see me and send a lightning bolt to shock my ass. Well, hate to break this to you, but Ted hardly watches what is going on here. Half the time, he is watching old Stallone and Brando movies; the other half of the time he spends with the ladies. He is one heck of a ladies' man. Think about it, who could resist a roll in the clouds with the big man himself? With the top dog always busy, never watching us, I can get away with pretty much anything. It also explains the state of the world.

The first audition was that Monday. It was a new musical that was going to be choreographed by Susan Stroman, so everyone was nervous. The waiting room was jam- packed with spandex-clad men (women's auditions were the next day) nervously talking to each other, having seen one another at countless auditions. Being new, I kept to myself, stretched, and did my vocal warm-ups. There were two parts of the audition—one was dance, the other vocal. Dance was first (since the lead needed to dance and sing, if you couldn't dance, you were out).

They called in ten of us at a time. They showed us a quick routine and gave us a few minutes to learn it. We then went into another room in front of the casting agents and did our dance. I admit that I wasn't on my best game, but I was, by far, not the worst in the room. I could have done better, but I was decent. After that it was back into the waiting room for another half hour. Then it was on to the singing. This I was more nervous about; it was a solo, meaning I had to go in alone. I made some new friends in the waiting room and they wished me luck.

This time, I was in front of different casting agents. I had to say my name and audition number and then sing. I chose to sing "One Song" from *Rent*; it's, like, my favorite song in the world and I can nail it. And nail it

I did. The second audition on Wednesday went about the same. I did well, but not my best. I didn't get either, but I wasn't discouraged. I made some new friends and they came over to my pad on 51st and Broadway that weekend for a small shindig. They were gay, but I didn't care; I love them guys. Oh, and that is another lie—if you're gay, it doesn't mean you end up with me. It's not really a sin anymore (well, originally it was going to be until Ted had a few too many one night at his annual birthday bash and had to change the rule, or he'd have been a hypocrite), so don't worry. We had a blast and they told me not to worry, that out of every hundred auditions I should only expect one callback.

And that is the way my life went for the next few months. Once a week, I'd drop in on hell and make my presence known, then I'd go back to audition. The rest of the time I spent going to bars and hanging out with my new friends. I even started to date a girl who worked on one of the shows. She was a stagehand, but it was still cool to hang out with someone in the "biz." Her name was Mary and she reminded me of Jesus' wife. Man, did they have a messed up relationship. He drank too much; his favorite line was "You hang on a cross and see if you don't drink!" When she got drunk, too, she would go over to Joseph's house a bit too late at night, though they always swore nothing ever happened. Whatever. Anyway, Mary introduced me to some people. It was a domino effect and, before I knew it, I had an in. I met the director, he liked me off the bat, and I nailed the audition. I got the part!

The ironic part of this story? The role I got was

for the *Jesus Christ Superstar* revival. I was to play Jesus. Talk about odd! Regardless, I didn't care what the role was. For the first time in my life, I was around people I liked, I was having fun, and I was happy. Rehearsal was long and tiring, yet thrilling. After six months, we opened for previews in Chicago and got great reviews. *Variety* called me "the next big thing to hit the Great White Way!" Another industry rag called me "Stan the Man."

It was the greatest time of my life. Out of the thousands of years I have lived, these few months were worth more than all of them. Opening night was a big to-do. We had celebrities lined up; the red carpet was rolled out. Every newspaper was there taking pictures as the cars arrived, and I was sitting backstage ready to throw up. Mary got a job on that show and she came into my dressing room beforehand to "calm me down" a bit. It worked. Everyone laughed at our situation, as well; here I was playing Jesus and my girl was named Mary.

When it was time for the curtain to go up, I was ready. This was it. We hit all of our marks. The show went off perfectly—no mess-ups and everyone was at the top of their game. During the standing ovation, I started to cry. I was so happy...

And that is when I saw him. Jesus was in the balcony, looking pissed. Obviously, he was drunk as hell; he threw a bottle at the stage, but it landed short and hit George Clooney in the back of the head, sending the audience into a panic.

Then, ignoring the rules of Earth, Jesus stepped off the balcony and floated towards the stage in his tux with a finger pointed at me. Some of the crowd screamed and ran, others thought it was part of the show. The cast just stood in awe. I braced myself, waiting for whatever the drunk was about to do to me. When he got two feet from me, just about to land on the stage, Mary came out of nowhere with a broom handle that she had snapped in half. It was jagged and pointy, pointy enough to go right through Jesus' gut. Shocked and confused, he forgot to levitate and fell into the orchestra pit. We took the opportunity to run.

Mary and I made it across the street and into a deli we frequented late nights. Scared, she asked what the hell was going on. I told her it was complicated. She gave me a look and told me that she had just stabbed someone with a broom; an explanation was needed. I told her I would tell her over drinks. After making sure the coast was clear, we made our way to Angus' for a drink. We got a seat in the back (after a few curious looks—I was still dressed as Jesus, after all) and ordered up some shots of Jack.

I told her the truth. I didn't know what else to say. She didn't believe me until I opened up a portal and had Mama T hand me some bubble gum. After that she was silent. I told her that I might only have a few minutes before they ripped me back to hell. It was then that I realized I loved her. I loved her more than Broadway and singing and performing. This was what was really missing in my life. Love. I grabbed her hand and told her I loved her, like I had many times before, but this time I knew she could tell I meant it with all my heart. Now, normally if a woman was told she was dating Satan, she might freak out. Not Mary. Instead, she pulled off my fake beard and kissed me.

Then she asked if I looked like this down under or if I looked like a monster, the way they always showed me on earth. I told her I looked like a normal human, though a bit better-looking than this. She laughed.

An hour later, I was still on earth and in Mary's bed. We had made love and we were both crying. And though I was thinking the same thing, it was Mary who brought the idea up: "What if I commit a major sin and got killed. Could we be together then? Forever?"

"Yes," was all I could say.

Within minutes, we were wandering the streets trying to find a bum. We found an elderly one that hardly looked alive. Mary didn't even hesitate; she took out the kitchen knife and plunged it into his chest four times. I couldn't help but smile. Afterwards, she kissed me and told me she'd see me in a few minutes. Then, she trotted off and jumped in front of a downtown bus.

The second she did this, I opened up my portal, jumped in, and waited for her. While I waited, I had John go out and find the bum that she had just killed and brought him to the front of the line. I explained the situation and told him he would have no punishment for eternity. He shook my hand and smiled as I had two bikini models escort him to his new apartment with a fully stocked bar. Ten minutes later, Mary was there. She didn't recognize me at first, but when she looked deep into my eyes she started to cry. I asked her if she could live with this face and she said, "Hell yes."

A week later, Ted reprimanded me for taking human form, but he didn't say much because his own son caused the biggest scandal on earth since Area 51 (which was actually caused by Ted's other son, Bob, who never made the good book because—let's just say he is, well, slow). He also went on to tell me that Jesus attended all productions of any show that had to do with him, even school productions. He just couldn't pass up seeing someone perform as him. With that, I was sent back to work.

That was three years ago. I now have a great wife and two children. And you know what? Work isn't that bad when you have family to come home to. And we plan to knock out a few more kids so we can start up a performing family, like the Osmond's, only of hell. That's my story of how I found love in hell, my friends. So come on down sometime. I'll be waiting for you.

Inspirations

WHITE ASH

Every morning, my wife and I turn on the news for a few minutes before we get out of bed. As we lay there groggily, we listen to the horrors that are going on in the world. One particular morning, there was a segment about how a twenty-year-old girl died when she slammed into a tree at three in the morning. It happens all the time, but when we heard that it was only two streets from our house, it made us sit up.

Later that day I drove by the tree where it happened. The bark was stripped away from where the car slammed into it, and there were dozens of flowers and candles around the trunk. I felt horrible, but then I noticed the house behind it. It was literally ten feet away. Someone's bedroom was ten feet away from where a car slammed into a tree and someone died. For some reason, I could not get that out of my head—not the girl dying, but what it must have been like to be the owners of that house.

They had to have woken up frightened; they had to have been the first ones to see the damage and...the dead girl. They had to put up with hordes of people on their front lawn, the news wanting to interview them. What was that like? With those thoughts in my head, I sat down to try and experience it. What it turned into is much more complicated than just a crash—but, at its heart, it's still about a family having to deal with a horrible situation.

THE EMPTY STOCKING

We all love a good Christmas story! Especially one that warms your heart and puts you in the mood for the holidays. Well, this story is not that. Personally, I love Christmas more than any other day. You could say I'm a jolly little elf. When it comes to writing, though, I'm not the sappy kind of guy. Personally, I like darker, more emotional things. With "The Empty Stocking," I knew I wanted to write a holiday story, only I didn't want to make it happy. That was the catalyst.

There is nothing sadder to me than the thought of being alone on Christmas. That thought is what started off the idea for this story. A man alone on the holidays. I tossed around some ideas in my head about a lonely man, but they all ended up being happy, like some made-for-TV movie where the man finds his true love on Christmas morning. For a while, I couldn't think of an idea; then, one afternoon, I was taking out some holiday decorations and held an empty stocking. It looked sad in my hands, all alone and flat.

I put the stocking on my writing desk and sat down. Staring at it, I suddenly got a wave of emotion and thought about what it would be like to have lost some family members on the holiday. That is when the idea sparked in my head. I sat down and started to type and wrote the story in one session. It seemed to come out naturally and, in edits, I didn't change much. The finished product is exactly what I wanted, the opposite of your typical holiday story.

WAKE UP STRONG

This story, which is a short insight into two people's minds before going to bed, came to me one night after I saw a very unhappy couple in a grocery store. As they put food into their carts, they looked like zombies. They hardly talked—the husband held up an item and the wife nodded yes or no. I followed them for a bit and watched how miserable they looked.

When I got home, I couldn't stop thinking about them as my wife told me a story about how one of her friends had gotten in another huge fight with her husband. This happened with that particular friend all the time. They fought because they didn't communicate. When my wife told me that the friend planned on getting pregnant, because she figured it would fix things between them, I couldn't believe it.

That night as I lay in bed, I thought about how well my wife and I communicated. We talked about everything, always. If I wasn't happy about something, I told her. We've only been together a few years, but we still laugh every day and hold hands every night. I'm very happy and the thought of turning into her friend or like the zombies I saw shopping earlier in the day baffles and frightens me. I tried to think what it would be like in a relationship with no communication, that lost its fire, and this quick story is what I came up with.

Stories come from anywhere. Fears, thoughts, things you see. This story came from all of those—something I saw, fears of losing what I have, and the thought of what it might be like. In your own writing, use everything you have. Watch people in public, use your friends and family as a springboard, and think about life, always.

THE PRIEST AND THE PLANE

There was a point in my life when I was flying constantly. I was actor and did appearances almost every single weekend. Usually, I would fly every Thursday and come back every Sunday night or Monday morning. There were times I was flying so much, I got to know some of the flight attendants and people working at the gates. At times, it was monotonous.

One of the things I used to fret about was getting a seat by myself. I'm a big guy, 6'2", so if I was on one of the small planes and had to sit next to someone, it was miserable. Obviously the main character, Jack, is the same way. The beginning of the story, when he watches people come in and hopes that no one will sit next to him, was my normal routine. On one particular flight, as I prayed that no one would sit next to me, a priest actually came and took the seat I was hoping would stay empty. I was miserable that I was going to have to be cramped for a few hours. Not only that, but in real life I am an atheist, and the idea of sitting next to a priest who might want to chat sent me in panic mode.

The old priest was friendly and tried a few times to start

211

conversation with me, but I stifled it with short answers. After a while, he gave up and went about reading his bible. I felt a bit rude, but I'm naturally shy and, even if he weren't a priest, I probably wouldn't have talked much more, anyway. As the flight took off and my legs started to cramp up, I started to think about the situation I was in. With my twisted mind, I started to wonder what would happen if the plane started to crash. Would the man want to take my hand and pray? Would he bless the plane and try to save us all?

As I sat and daydreamed, the story unfolded in my mind. When I got home, I started to write it and removed myself from the equation. Obviously, the story has a pro-religious and mystical ending. Though I am an atheist, I love the idea and magic behind religion. I wanted to put the character—and, in turn, myself—in a situation he couldn't understand to see what would happen, and that is where the ending came from.

PEBBLES

The inspiration for this story has a rather simple explanation. I decided to take the plunge and propose to my girlfriend. Her mother gave me the family diamond and I had a ring custom-made. With the ring in hand, I was emotionally ready to ask her; the only problem was, I needed to figure out a way how. Being a performer at heart, I wanted to do something big. I threw around dozens of ideas that ranged from skydiving onto her work to placing a television ad. Then, one day, I jokingly said to her that if I ever proposed, I would do it in a big way. She freaked. She really doesn't like the spotlight, so the thought of having dozens of people around watching her answer didn't make her too happy. I had to rethink my ideas.

The thought of proposing over a fancy dinner wasn't to appealing to me, so I sat holding the ring one day and tried to think of ways to ask her that would be out of the limelight. That was when the idea of taking a hike came into my mind. We weren't big hikers, but I knew I could get her to go on one without any suspicion. I liked the idea; I could make it romantic and secluded, just like in the story. I was getting excited when, suddenly, I got the image off her falling off a cliff as she looked at the ring. She is a bit clumsy. Soon as I saw that image of her falling, I knew I wasn't going to ask her on a cliff—yet the idea someone proposing and then falling down a cliff was intriguing to me. I put the ring in its box and moved to my computer.

A few hours later I had an outline of what would become "Pebbles."

If you're wondering, I did propose and we have been happily married for some time now, though my proposal didn't go as planned. I still hadn't figured out what I wanted to do when, all of a sudden, I felt pressured to ask her. Everyone in her family and mine knew I was going to do it and they were all hoping I would do it before her family reunion so we could celebrate it. The night before I decided to do it, I was going to ask her next to a pond that we visited on a regular basis to feed the ducks. It was beautiful and peaceful at sunset. I was all set, but I couldn't get her to go for a walk. I asked several times, tried to talk her into it, but she wasn't up for it. Flustered, I didn't know what to do; the ring was burning a hole in my pocket and I didn't want anyone at the reunion to spill the beans. Before we went to bed, she asked why I was acting all weird. In a panic I dropped to my knee and asked her in our bedroom. She said it was perfect, but I still would have rather skydived in.

On a separate note, something eerie happened shortly after I posted this story. Exactly what I wrote happened. A real-life couple went for a hike, the man proposed, and the woman got so excited she fell off the cliff! Thankfully, their story had a better outcome: they both lived.

LADYBUG

It seems like we can't go a month now without a work or school shooting. They are horrible and I never understand them. Why would you want to take out innocent people that have done nothing to you?

One day, I was sitting at my writing desk with CNN on. I was ignoring the broadcast and working on my website when they suddenly made a big huff about breaking news. Of course, I stopped and looked up. It was a workplace shooting. I sighed, not really wanting to watch it, but CNN is addictive. The glow of the TV drew me away from my desk and closer to it. For the next two hours, I watched the live coverage as if it were the Super Bowl. When it was over and they finally started taking commercial breaks, I went back to my desk and sulked.

Thinking about these shooters, I wondered how they could get to that point. In deep thought, my gaze wandered outside. It was peaceful. I imagined sitting out on the grass, in the calm peacefulness, knowing that my life was over, like those shooters. It was then that I started to write. I think I wrote because I wanted to feel that moment of calm before it was all over. Unlike the

216

shooter on the news, I didn't want to kill my character; I wanted him to pay for it. Getting shot is too easy of a way out; spending the rest of your life in jail, now that is a punishment.

FALLING STAR

A while back, a news article came out about how there was a silent, black and white sex film of Marilyn Monroe. Supposedly, the film showed Marilyn giving oral to a man whose face you never see. The FBI owned this video, which led most people to speculate that the man in it was President Kennedy. The fifteen-minute-long film went up for auction. It ended up selling to a private collector for 1.5 million dollars. When I read that article, for some reason it intrigued me.

For a while, I thought about how interesting it would be to find something like that of a famous celebrity. That is when the seed of the story started. At first, the idea was just to have someone find old pictures or a film in an estate sale. The idea didn't grab me enough, though. That is when I asked myself, *What if someone kept things, but didn't want to get rid of them because they meant something to him?* The story formed from
there.

I needed a situation where the owner knew about the items and kept them hidden, but would eventually have them discovered. That was when the story fully formed.

Why not make it an old star that fell and became nothing?
After that realization, the story came together rather
quickly.

JUST KILLING TIME

In my old apartment complex in Oklahoma, I had a great writing room. It was technically the sunroom, but I used it as my office, sitting there for hours per day writing. It had floor-to-ceiling windows all around and a corner fireplace. It was beautiful and peaceful, though as a writer, I believe windows can be a gift and a curse. Some days, I had to have all the blinds shut, as I would look out the windows and watch the world, getting no work done. Then again, other days, the things I saw would inspire me.

The complex was a series of buildings, three stories high with balconies. Across from my windows I could see a series of balconies. Some had elaborate outdoor furniture, lights, and decorations. The bottom one, however, had a solo lawn chair. There were days when I would see no activity on that sad balcony. Then there were days when I would see an old man sitting there for hours on end. Some days he would read books, and others he would just sit and stare and say hello to whomever walked by. It broke my heart how lonely he looked.

There were only a few children in the complex. One of them was a little girl who would ride her pink bike in a loop around the sidewalk, circle after circle, day after day. She looked just as lonely as the old man. She would wave to the old man and he would nod, but they never talked, never had any other communication that I saw. Some days, I found myself holding my breath as she circled past his balcony, hoping she would stop and they would chat. It never happened.

Their loneliness depressed me, so I decided to put them together in a story. The first draft was not in the form of a letter and, when I started it, I had no clue what was going to happen in the end. All I knew was that I wanted them to have a friendship, which they do in the story, but for some reason I couldn't make it a happy story. I found it becoming dark as it progressed and, finally, ironic. We moved away not long after I wrote this and I have no idea whether the old man ever befriended the girl, but in my mind I like to think he did, and I like to think it turned out better than in my story.

HOW DO YOU?

The shortest story in this collection has the shortest origin. The story idea came out after I heard about a young father dying. He had a heart attack at thirty-six, leaving behind three children under seven years old. A death like that is tragic, but for some reason, all I could think was, "How do you tell the children?" It was that simple idea that inspired me to write this very, very short story.

V.A.M.P

Ask teens right now what their favorite book is, and most likely they will say *Twilight*. The four-book series about sparkly vampires has become one of the most successful series in decades—so much so it has inspired dozens of vampire knockoffs. Of course, vampire stories have been around for centuries and have enjoyed varying peaks of success. It was during the peak of the *Twilight* craze that this story came to mind. The reason, I was sick of seeing vampire books everywhere I went!

Originally, I set out to write a satire like "Stan the Man", but as it got going it took on a semi-serious tone. The first draft was written with a much more humorous tone. There was the tiny bookend of the character wanting to be with his love. On the second reading, I realized that it could be more powerful, so I took out some of the humor and molded it into what it is today.

In fact, by the time I wrote the final draft, I realized that this was something I might turn into a novel. As of now, I think it works as a stand-alone piece, but if I ever wanted to, I could easily use it as an introduction to a novel. Maybe someday I will; only time will tell.

A FLOWER FOR MAE

I'm an avid jogger. Usually, I run five days a week and, depending on the season and my shape, I go anywhere from two to twenty miles. Running is my drug of choice. It clears my head and gives me ideas for my stories. One day, I was running outside near my parents' home in Massachusetts. I was about two miles out, on what I consider a dangerous stretch of road with no sidewalks, when I saw a small boy riding his bicycle. I'm a grown man and running that particular stretch made me nervous; the child, who was no more than eight years old, definitely should not have been riding his bike there. We were heading in opposite directions. When he got close to me, I stopped my jog and pulled off my headphones. I stepped onto the grass to give him room to pass. I tried to stop him to ask what he was doing, but he didn't look at me; he had a look of determination on his face like I had never seen before. As he passed, I kept my eye on him until he made it to a sidewalk.

Relieved, I continued my jog.

For the rest of the jog, I couldn't help but think of the kid. I was worried he was going to get hit by a car, but mostly I wondered why he would be riding his bike on such a dangerous road. At that age, I wasn't allowed to leave the driveway, let alone the street. Even after I got home and showered, I couldn't get that kid's face out of my mind. He looked like he was on a mission, a mission he was going to accomplish no matter what. I tried to think about being that age—what would be so important? A toy? A friend? Then I thought about how I was a baby Casanova, always in love and flirting with women three times my age. What if the kid was in love with his teacher? What if he was trying to get something to impress her? From there, I had my jumping off point and the story unfolded. Of course, I couldn't help but put myself in as the jogger!

A HAPPY STORY

If you have read a lot of my stuff, you probably know that I tend to write darker things. There usually aren't too many happy endings and, almost always, someone dies. I can't help it; I like the dark side of society, mostly because I can't fathom doing or dealing with most of the things in my stories. I find a lover falling off a cliff on what should be the happiest day of her life much more interesting than her having a romantic evening on the cliff and living happily ever after. It's the dark side I like and write about often. On the other hand, my wife, mother, and several friends love sappy, romantic, "happy" stories. After one particular unhappy story, I got bombarded with people saying, "For once, can't you just write a happy story?" After the third person in one day said that to me, I decided to try it out.

Seriously, I sat down with every intention to write an upbeat story. I had no clue what I was going to write, so I created a document, titled it "A Happy Story" (planning to change it later), and then stared at the blank screen. I racked my brains for something romantic and loving that would move the women in my life. I thought of every Nicholas Sparks movie I had ever seen and I still came up with nothing. Giving up, I worked on some other stuff and decided to tackle "A Happy Story" later, hoping something would come to me. Nothing did. The next day, I was just as blank.

Frustrated that I couldn't think of a romantic short story, I decide to write a fictionalized version of what I was going through. What resulted is a story about a writer, trying to write a happy story for his mother and, in the end, he dies. So I didn't accomplish what I set out to do, but at the same time, it is something I love much more than a happy ending!

I never did write my mother and wife a happy story, but who knows? Maybe I will someday—as long as I can kill someone in it!

THE QUADRIPLEGIC
AND THE BOAT

This is probably the simplest explanation for a story idea in this book. I was watching TV, clicking around, and caught a few seconds of *What Lies Beneath*. There is a scene in the movie where Harrison Ford uses a drug on Michele Pfeiffer that makes her unable to move. I remember watching it in the theater and feeling that insane uneasiness at the thought of not being able to move. For some reason, that terrifies me. Not being able to move, but able to think…gives me the willies.

As I watched a few minutes of that movie I thought about that horrible feeling and it stuck in my head. I ended up wanting to do my own version of that concept. With the idea of not being able to move at hand, I began tossing around some ideas. I decided quickly that I did not want a good person suffering with immobility, so I made the character a killer. That way, being alone, trapped in his mind was his punishment. From there, I needed a setting that would be harsh to the character—a house or street didn't work. Not much would happen and he would probably be found quickly. When the idea of a boat popped in my head, the story fell into place rather quickly.

This ended up being, arguably, my favorite story in the collection.

Michael Aloisi

THE MISADVENTURES OF A BABY-KILLING BOYFRIEND

This is probably the most bizarre story in the collection. "Misadventures" is one of the first times I stepped out of my comfort zone of serious writing and attempted humor. Though it seems like nothing that would ever come from an MFA program, I actually wrote this while pursuing my degree. To the horror of everyone, I work-shopped it into one of my classes. At first, everyone turned their noses up at the idea of a white trash idiot trying to kill his girlfriend's baby, but they eventually enjoyed it, as it was a break from the more "serious" writing.

As for where this idea came from: I have a sick, dark sense of humor (that goes along with my writing). My girlfriend at the time, (who later became my wife) casually asked what would happen if she got pregnant. Without hesitation, I jokingly said I would push her down the stairs. When she replied, "No, seriously," I answered by saying I would slip some bleach into her water bottle. For some odd reason, she did not find this funny. When she asked a third time, I racked my brain trying to think of a way to abort a baby without her knowing so I could have another zinger for an answer. It was then that the light bulb went off. I was making jokes, but how funny would it be if a man actually did try to kill his girlfriend's baby over and over again, but kept messing up? As I started to think of a story, my girlfriend sighed and gave up on our conversation. Thankfully, she wasn't actually pregnant.

With the concept in my brain, I needed a character that was so dumb he would actually want to try and kill his girlfriend's baby and keep messing it up. That was when Ricky crawled into my brain. A moronic "white trash" stereotype was perfect for the situation. With the character in mind, all the pieces started to fall into place. The funny thing is, as despicable as Ricky was, I was having fun beating him up over and over again, which is probably why the story became one of my longer shorts.

With the characters and concepts in place, it wasn't hard thinking of ridiculous situations for him. Even though I work-shopped the piece, the final draft didn't change much from the first one. I knew what I wanted and hit it pretty much on the head the first try. Who knows, maybe Ricky will pop up again sometime in another "Misadventure."

A MODERN DAY ROMANCE

"A Modern Day Romance" is my take on the digital dating world. During my years in New York City, I was a bit of a recluse. Every day, I would go out into the city, go shopping, go to movie, and get meals—yet I wouldn't really have any human interaction. I was a bit of a loner in a city of millions. I was a writer. Being lonely, I turned to online dating.

Now this isn't a promotion of online dating, but because I am a shy person, I loved it. I got to meet women I would never have met in my daily life. I got to see what they looked like and get to know them before I ever had to meet them in real life. By the time I met them, I felt like I knew everything about them. It was like meeting an old friend, not a stranger. I could write an entire book on my dating adventures, but again, this is not what this is about.

It wasn't until years after my online dating was over and I was living with my future wife that I started to think back on those days, after I saw a news article about how 40 million people were online dating. I thought about how many people I talked to online for months, yet never met.

It was then that I realized you could have a whole relationship without ever actually meeting the person.

When I started writing, I knew I wanted to have two people meet, fall in love, and break up, all via email. The story started from there. It went through several drafts, as I was in my MFA program at the time and I work-shopped. It changed from the man being a player and getting caught in the end (emailing her and a dozen other women at the same time) to what it is now: a woman who gets scared off by the looks of a man, even though she thinks he is great.

As of now I believe the concept is great, but this story doesn't hit the nail on the head. One day in the future, I may try to give this another whack, but as of now, I think it's cute and I like it.

DOODY DUTY

We have all stepped in a pile of dog crap once or twice in our life. Of course, stepping in a steaming heap was the inspiration for this story. I was living in a beautiful apartment complex in Oklahoma, one of those private, gated types that have hot tubs, gyms, and all sorts of free stuff for residents. It was a lovely place with a lot of rules to ensure life was good there. But one rule was not followed: picking up after your dog.

There were nice courtyards throughout the complex; I would walk down the paths to the gym every day. It was a nice walk until I stepped in dog crap one morning. I was annoyed but didn't think much of it (after I cleaned it off, that is). A week later, when I had new $150 running shoes, I stepped in another pile. It sent me over the edge; I was furious, but there wasn't anything I could do. Later that day, I was sitting in my writing studio staring out the window, contemplating a story. A young woman was walking her dog. Because she was the only thing moving out there, I watched her. The dog squatted a few yards from my door, did his business, and the lady just walked away, not cleaning it up. I'm not the sort of person that confronts people, so I didn't run out and yell at her like I wanted to.

Over the next few days, I watched as dozens of people did not clean up after their dogs. I was furious, but couldn't really do anything about it. To get that anger out, I started a story. I took stepping in dog crap to the extreme, made the consequences big and the revenge even bigger. Through my writing, I got my revenge on the lazy people in my complex. After writing the story, I wasn't as mad anymore, though I did watch my step more carefully! This is a perfect example of how writing can be therapeutic.

The funny thing is that I completely made up the company at the end, Doody Duty. I had no clue that a dog cleanup service even existed. When one was pointed out to me, I did some research. I couldn't believe how many there were! I even found one with the same name I made up. Sometimes creativity and the real world collide!

This is another example of how you can take a situation in your life and turn it into a story. Next time you step in a pile of crap, take that anger and create your own story.

TOOTH FAIRY INFLATION

Walking through a store one day, I saw a little kid with his hand deep in his mouth. I watched for a few seconds and quickly determined that he was trying to pull out a loose tooth. The mother finally saw him and slapped his hand away. I couldn't really hear what he said, but I did catch *tooth fairy*. It made me think about how excited I was to lose a tooth myself at that age. And that is where the story began.

All I knew was I wanted to write something about a kid losing her first tooth. Then I thought about the parents, having to sneak in and steal the tooth to replace it with money (sorry to ruin it for you who still believe, but the tooth fairy doesn't exist); it would be just as new and exciting to them. I wondered how much a tooth is worth nowadays? I used to get a few dollars, but with inflation and all... With that last thought, the story tumbled into place.

OBAMA WILL NOT SCARE ME

Despite its title, implying anti-Obama sentiment, *Obama Will Not Scare Me* is a rather light, quirky effort of mine. The idea came up when I was visiting my father's work one day (he runs an old paper mill). I was walking through the office after-hours with my dad, who wanted to show me some changes they had made. We assumed no one was there, as it was after hours. While my dad went to the bathroom, I walked around curiously looking at offices and displays. I went into a dark room, snapped on the light, and, bam, there was Obama! I grasped my chest and thought I was going to have a heart attack at the ripe old age of twenty-nine. When I realized it was a cutout of Obama, I started to laugh hysterically.

When my father came out, I told him about it. He didn't laugh; he didn't find the cutout funny at all. Being in charge of the mill meant that if there was a burglar alarm, my father was called in; he has to walk the floors to make sure everything is fine. At two in the morning, walking the dark floors to see if there was a burglar—well, this cutout would definitely be fodder for a heart attack. Especially since my dad said they were dressing it up and moving it around the office almost every day since the inauguration.

Finally, it got to the point where my father declared that it had to be set in one location, for his sake.

I found this whole situation hysterical. For one, a cutout spooking you is laughable, but your President making you scream, even better. I couldn't get that cardboard Obama out of my head for a few days. It was then that I started to think about a story. At first, I was going to use my father as the main character, checking on a burglar alarm, but I quickly realized I needed someone who would run into the cutout day after day, alone. Who better than a janitor, alone in the offices at night!

At first, I had no clue what the outcome would be. All I had was a guy getting scared over and over again. Then "The Boy Who Cried Wolf" popped into my head. The fake scare needed to turn real. When I realized this, the rest of the story just came out. The ending did change, though. In the first draft, he just stopped a burglar. During a second read, I decided it wasn't enough; I needed it to go farther. That was when I put in the element of him stopping a terrorist and getting an award for saving the lives of citizens.

This story is just another example of how you can use your daily life to come up with an idea. A normal person would have gotten startled by the cutout, laughed, and never thought about it again. As a writer, though, you need to take your experience and turn them into stories.

RUDOLPH, THE LATER YEARS

It was during a guest lecture that I got the idea for "Rudolph, the Later Years." I was asked to give a talk and then join the class for their usual routine. After the lecture, the class settled in to do a writing exercise. The teacher, a friend of mine and a fellow writer, passed out several small Christmas-themed cartoons (it was late December). The assignment was to pick one of them and write a story about it for five minutes. The cartoon I picked was of a drunken reindeer. The teacher had cut off the captions, so we only had the pictures.

Staring at the picture, I thought of my favorite holiday classic, *Rudolph, the Red-Nosed Reindeer.* I grew up watching it every holiday and it was near and dear to my heart. Seeing that drunken reindeer, I couldn't help but wonder if it was Rudolph. Now, I never write freehand—I have horrible writing and can't read it afterwards—so it was hard for me to scribble out a story in five minutes, though I did get a few paragraphs down. The class went around reading their stories. When it was my turn, I stumbled over my bad handwriting, but the students enjoyed it nonetheless. I thought it was cute, but closed my notebook and didn't think anything of it.

When I moved almost a year later, I was going through stuff and found the notebook. I read it over, thought it was cute, and, because it was near Christmastime again, I decided to give it another shot. I typed up the few paragraphs I had and then edited and expanded them into what the story is now.

There is nothing remarkable about the creation of this story, but for budding writers, it should serve as a good lesson: never throw out anything you write., no matter how short or how bad you think it is. Keep all your writing. You never know—you may want to revisit it or read it years later and realize it was actually pretty good. It also goes to show that a story can come out of a typical writing exercise.

STAN THE MAN

Come on, who didn't know that Satan wanted to be a Broadway star? I mean, it's common sense. Wait a minute...

The idea for this story came from an urge to write a satire about the devil. Why I had that urge, I have no clue. I just remember having the idea to write a story that the devil himself was telling, but I didn't want it to be dark and creepy. I wanted it to be funny. When I sat down to write, that was all I had in mind. I didn't know he would want to be on Broadway or end up performing *Jesus Christ Superstar*! Through the magic of writing, it just sort of happened.

Though I'm not a big fan of comedic writing, I do like satire. I like taking things and turning them on their head to see the lighter side. Think about it—if you believe in hell and Satan, then you think he is the most evil horrible thing in the world. So what better than to write about him in the opposite light?

241

ACKNOWLEDGEMENTS

I'd like to thank some people for their help with this book. First and foremost, my wife for supporting my writing career, without her cheering me on I wouldn't be able to create anything. Of course I'd like to thank my Mom, Dad, brother, Aunt Lorraine and Uncle Tom for all being so supportive of my writing career over the years.

I'd also like to thank Meredith Dias for editing the book. It takes a brave person to take on my atrocious spelling and grammar! Lastly I'd like to thank Sarah M. W. Espano and the Enve Creative team for helping with the design of the cover and creating the *AuthorMike Ink* logo.

White Ash
Audio Book

Now that you have read the book, listen to the audio version! Available on CD or for digital download. Each story is introduced by music and read by the author himself, who brings life to the stories by giving different characters their own voices.

To purchase the audio version, search *White Ash* or *Michael Aloisi* at online retailers such as Amazon.com, iTunes, AuthorMike.com or visit your favorite online retailer!

Created by author Michael Aloisi, *Ink* is an independent publishing company that focuses on writers and readers. Honoring its motto of *"Passion, not profit,"* *Ink* is dedicated to producing high-quality books that traditional publishers might not take a risk on. Traditional publishers will not take risks on books unless they know they will make a profit; Ink takes those risks to reward readers and writers by getting exciting fiction into reader's hands.

Visit Ink's website to see more of its releases and learn how you can submit your own stories.

AuthorMikeInk.com

Fifty Handfuls
By
Michael Aloisi

After years of hard work, Kathleen (Kat) Cutter has been offered her dream job. Only one thing is holding her back: she has just found out that she's pregnant. Kat suddenly finds herself torn between choosing her dream job or fulfilling her husband Jasper's dream of becoming a father.

When Jasper is found dead and she loses the baby, Kat has nothing to live for—until she finds a crayon-written contract between Jasper and herself that reminds her of a promise she intends to keep. She sets off cross-country alone, with nothing but Jasper's ashes to help her conquer her emotions, a stalker, and the rest of the crazy world. She's determined to keep her word.

Even if it kills her.

Mr. Bluestick
By
Michael Aloisi

Imaginary friends. Everyone's had them. They're harmless products of childhood. But what if your child's imaginary friend wasn't imaginary?

Worrywart father Tom Boyer has just found the perfect home for his family: a bigger house in a better neighborhood, with woods in the back where his daughter, Lilly, can play. But the move has been tough on Lilly; there are no kids on the street for Lilly to play with. So when she finds a fascinating friend in Mr. Bluestick, a mysterious man who wears a tuxedo and carries a glowing blue cane while living in the woods, Tom is amused—until he awakens one night with the woods on fire and Lilly missing.

AuthorMike

Be sure to visit Michael Aloisi's website to read new monthly short stories and articles, listen to audio shorts, read interviews with Mike, and learn about his classes and lectures. You can drop Mike a line or invite him to your local book club, library, bookstore, or school. While you're on the site, don't forget to add him to your favorite social networking pages!

www.AuthorMike.com

CPSIA information can be obtained at www.ICGtesting.com
Printed in the USA
BVOW040350170513

320969BV00001B/6/P